D0380754

9/10

Hard Ride

CALGARY PUBLIC LIBRARY

AUG - - 2015

ALSO BY OPAL CAREW

Bliss
Forbidden Heat
Secret Ties
Six
Blush
Swing
Twin Fantasies
Pleasure Bound
Total Abandon
Secret Weapon
Insatiable
Illicit
His to Command
His to Possess
His to Claim
Riding Steele

Hard Ride

Opal Carew

ST. MARTIN'S GRIFFIN
NEW YORK

This is a work of fiction. All of the characters, organizations, and events portrayed in this novel are either products of the author's imagination or are used fictitiously.

HARD RIDE. Copyright © 2015 by Opal Carew. All rights reserved. For information, address St. Martin's Press, 175 Fifth Avenue, New York, N.Y. 10010.

www.stmartins.com

Library of Congress Cataloging-in-Publication Data

Carew, Opal.
    Hard ride : a ready to ride novel / Opal Carew. — First edition.
        pages ; cm. — (Ready to ride ; 4)
    ISBN 978-1-250-05283-4 (trade paperback)
    ISBN 978-1-4668-5469-7 (e-book)
    1. Man-woman relationships—Fiction.   2. Sexual dominance and submission—Fiction.   I. Title.
    PR9199.4.C367H37 2015
    813'.6—dc23

                                                    2015016279

St. Martin's Griffin books may be purchased for educational, business, or promotional use. For information on bulk purchases, please contact the Macmillan Corporate and Premium Sales Department at 1-800-221-7945, extension 5442, or write to specialmarkets@macmillan.com.

First Edition: July 2015

10 9 8 7 6 5 4 3 2 1

To the Pub-Craft team,
such a lovely and wonderful group of people:
Laurie, Tim, Bharath, Monique, and Marissa.
Thank you all for your love and support!

Acknowledgments

Thank you, Rose Hilliard, for your unwavering faith in me. Thank you, Emily Sylvan Kim, for always believing in me. Thanks to Mark, Matt, and Jason, the three special men in my life, for always being there for me. And thank you, Laurie, who makes me feel I can accomplish anything!

Part One

Liv sipped her drink as she glanced around the bar, her heartbeat racing. Carl said he would meet her here at midnight and it was now close to one. She glanced toward the bar and the big, scary-looking tattooed guy who kept staring at her.

He saw her glancing his way and smiled, then stood up and started walking toward her table.

She turned away, keeping him in her peripheral vision, hoping he would be discouraged by her lack of interest. But no such luck. He grabbed one of the empty chairs at her table and turned it around, then sat down on it backward.

"Hey, babe. You look pretty lonely sitting here all by yourself."

She turned to face him. His dark, unsettling gaze locked on her.

"A pretty little lady like you shouldn't be all alone. Me and my men would be happy to offer our company."

The scraping of other chairs drew her attention as three

other guys sat down. They plunked their half-drunk beer bottles on the table.

"I'm not alone. I'm meeting someone here," she said.

"Really?" He glanced around. "I don't see no one." He glanced at the burly-bearded guy to his left. "Hawg, do you see anyone?"

Hawg shook his head. "No, sir, Crow, I don't see no one."

Crow leaned close to her, his sour beer breath enough to make her want to vomit. "I think maybe you're lyin' to us. You bin sittin' here for near an hour and no one's come by." He scratched his raspy chin and glanced at the others. "I think maybe the lady thinks she's too good for us."

"I think you're right, Crow," the tall man who sat across the table from him said. He had a ring in his nose and a tattoo along each side of his neck.

"Hey, leave the woman alone or I'm callin' the cops again."

Liv glanced up thankfully at the bartender, who'd stepped to her rescue.

"Danny, why don't you just stay out of it? It's no skin off your nose if—"

"Shut it, Crow," Danny said, cutting off his words. "If you don't want me banning you from here for good, then get lost. You're cut off anyway."

Crow scowled, but pushed himself to his feet. "Whatever."

The others followed him to the door and they left.

"Look," Danny the bartender said, "I don't need you coming in here, causing trouble with my regulars."

"But I didn't do anything."

His gaze slid down her body, then back up, and he har-rumphed. "Yeah, right." Then he turned and walked away.

Anger seethed through her. All she did was sit in a bar and be female and she was blamed for the actions of those oafs?

She'd long ago realized that life wasn't fair, but she hated being reminded of it.

She settled the bill and stood up.

Shock stared across the bar at the woman sitting alone at the table. She had big eyes, a small, heart-shaped mouth, and honey-blonde hair that floated in waves over her shoulders.

"Ah, fuck," he said as recognition hit him.

Wild Card glanced around from his conversation with Magic and Dom. "What is it?"

"I know that woman," he said. And, as usual, she was somewhere she shouldn't be, probably causing all kinds of trouble.

He'd watched as the men approached the single woman sitting at the table, ready to lurch to her aid. She clearly hadn't wanted their attention, but Danny had stepped in before things had gone too far.

If Shock had known it was Liv, though, he would have been at her side in the blink of an eye. As much as he re-sented her rejection in college, it didn't change the intense protectiveness he'd always felt for her.

She stood up and headed for the door.

"Guys, let's go," Shock said.

"I'm not finished with my beer," Magic complained.

"Now," Shock said.

Magic grumbled, but tipped back his bottle and downed what was left. So did Wild Card and Dom, then all of them stood and followed Shock out the back door, to where their bikes were parked.

Once out on the street, which was pretty deserted at this time of night, Liv started walking down the road. She wanted to grab a cab, but there were no cars at all on this road right now. After a few minutes of walking, heading toward a busier street, she started to get nervous. It was at times like this she wished she still had her car, but with the drain on her finances, it was a luxury she could no longer afford.

There were some men hanging out on the corner ahead. Rough-looking men. Maybe she should go back inside and have the bartender call her a cab.

She turned and started to walk back, but as she got close to the bar, a few more rough-looking types exited the bar and started walking toward her. Their gazes locked on her.

Her stomach clenched and a chill quivered through her.

Damn Carl for leaving her stranded here. Ordinarily, she would never come to a place like this, especially alone, but Carl had insisted the only time he could meet her was after his shift as a bouncer at a nearby bar.

She turned down an alley beside her. She was pretty sure it led to the next block and she could probably catch a cab there. Or at least slip into the all-night diner she'd seen on the way here this evening.

But as she walked down the dimly lit alleyway, she wondered if she'd made a grave mistake. She couldn't see very far ahead, but shouldn't she see streetlights from the next block? Or headlights of cars driving by?

She heard a sound behind her and glanced over her shoulder as she picked up her pace. Her breath caught at the shadowy shapes of three men behind her. She lurched forward and ran smack into a big, solid body. She gasped as she pushed herself back from a man with a broad, muscular chest and thick, tattooed arms.

Oh, God, the guy from the bar.

She gazed up at him, expecting to see the leering face of the man called Crow, but her eyes widened. In the dim light of the alley, she couldn't make out much of his face, but this tall stranger wasn't Crow or any of the men who'd been with him.

He grasped her arms and propelled her backward toward the building, then she felt the brick wall at her back. All she could see of his face was the steely glint of his eyes. Her heart pounded.

"Do you really think it's a good idea to be walking through a dark alley alone at night?" His words came out low and fierce.

Tears threatened at the dire situation she found herself in, but something about his voice nagged at her. There was something about it that was . . . familiar.

He leaned in closer. "But you always were lacking in common sense."

Shock vaulted through her. That was it. That voice unmistakably belonged to—

"Devin?"

He tightened his hold on her shirt, pushing her harder against the wall, anger emanating from him, so volatile she knew he was using his impressive self-control to suppress it. But she sensed it could explode at any time.

"What are you doing here?" she asked.

"No, you don't ask me questions," he flared. "You're the one in a dangerous situation. I ask the questions. What are *you* doing here?"

His tight grip on her loosened a little, and the short, raspy breaths she was sucking in slowed down. She took a deep intake of air to calm herself down.

"What was it?" he went on. "A dare? You never could resist those."

She frowned, annoyed at him for bringing up the way she'd been when she was in college. A lot had happened since then, and she was much more responsible now. He didn't know that. After they'd parted ways, he'd probably gone back to his rich family, taken control of the business, and become a big hotshot CEO. Not that she'd heard anything about him. He traveled in different circles than she did.

Of course, he always had. Even when they'd known each other in college. He had money, family connections, everything. She'd worked for everything she had. But Mr. Devin Ancaster had never understood that. He was from a completely different world.

"I was supposed to meet someone here," she said.

It was unsettling being this close to him. The old attraction flared in her despite the fact she thought she'd left those feelings behind a long time ago.

His eyebrow arched. "Your boyfriend suggested you meet him here? You should dump him."

She scowled. "He's not my boyfriend."

The warmth of his big body so close to her kept her senses reeling. If only he would step back and give her some breathing space.

He shrugged. "Whatever. Whoever he is, you shouldn't trust someone who suggests you come somewhere like this, especially late at night."

"Don't tell me who I should and shouldn't trust," she snapped. "It's my life and I've been taking care of it just fine without your help, thank you very much."

The steel in his eyes eased a little and he stepped back. The tension in her body dissipated as he gave her more space.

"How did you plan to get home? Is your car nearby?"

"No, I was going to get a cab."

"I'll take you."

"You don't need to do that. I can make my own way home." She glanced around the alley, wondering how to get to a busy street from here. But the thought of walking through the alley, then down the street where she remembered the men hanging out at the corner, made her nervous.

"But . . . maybe you could just walk me to where I can find a cab."

"So you're actually willing to accept some help from me?"

Annoyance flickered through her. "If it's a problem . . ."

He grasped her arm and hooked it around his elbow. "Not at all."

Devin led her back to the street where the other three men, who she'd noticed behind her earlier, still stood. She'd forgotten all about them.

"You know those men?" she asked as they got closer to them.

"Liv, these are my friends. Wild Card, Magic, and Dom."

They all stepped onto the well-lit street again. They were all tough-looking men wearing heavy biker boots, jeans, and T-shirts; their arms well muscled and inked.

The one named Wild Card grinned. He was the shortest of the men at about six foot two, with hazel eyes and dark blond hair spiked on top and short on the sides.

He held out his hand and she shook it. He had a tattoo the length of his left arm, swirls of blue, purple, and red surrounding three stars.

Magic had dark brown hair that was combed back like James Dean. The sleeves of his T-shirt had been torn off, revealing arms just as bulging and inked as his friends'. He shook her hand with a firmer grip and she noticed that the thorny vine tattooed on his arm extended under the shirt at the shoulder and coiled around his wrist. The way the thorns were inked, they seemed to penetrate his skin, complete with drops of blood.

Dom, who was the tallest, offered his hand next. Both his arms were covered with thick, black Celtic tattoos. A one-inch scar slashed across his chin, partially covered by the fringe of hair that formed a line along the edge of his chin from temple to temple. His big fingers enveloped hers and she felt power emanating from him. He was strong, with a potent masculinity, and she felt deep in her bones that he would always be in control in any relationship with a woman, but that woman would be totally safe and protected with him.

Which was how she'd always felt with Devin.

She turned to look at Devin again, and was jolted by the sight of him. Gone was the young man who'd always projected an image of casual elegance in expensive designer clothes that accentuated his clean-cut good looks. Now he wore the same type of attire as the others, and from his biker boots, faded, well-worn jeans, and T-shirt stretched taut over his muscular chest, to his unshaven face and unkempt hair, he was every bit the badass biker.

It didn't change how exceptionally handsome he was, though. If anything, the way his thick, dark brown hair combined with the scruffy whiskers on his face gave his chiseled good looks a rugged edge.

He even had tattoos. On one bicep he had two dragons within the boundaries of a star frame, and on the other, what looked like a newly added tribal armband, judging from the trace of redness.

"Liv's an old friend from college," Devin told them.

"Any friend of Shock's is a friend of ours," Wild Card said.

"Shock?" She glanced at Devin.

"That's what people know me as now," Devin said.

"That's his ride name," Magic said. "Now"—he grinned—"what did you say his real name is?"

"She didn't," Devin said, sending her a stare that made it clear he didn't want her telling them.

She pursed her lips, the rebel in her considering telling them right now, but why make him angry? Especially since she did want him to walk her to a taxi.

"If he says his name is Shock, then that's what it is."

Magic laughed. "Spoilsport."

"I'm walking Liv to a taxi," Devin said. "I'll see you back at the house later."

"Okay, man," Dom said. "But I'd have Liv check her wallet first."

Liv frowned, then dug through her purse looking for her red leather wallet. "Oh, my God, my wallet's gone."

Dom shrugged. "They've had a problem with pickpockets at Matey's Bar."

"How did you know where I was?" she asked.

"We saw you in there," Devin answered. "And I saw those guys badgering you. That's why we came out to see if you were okay."

His words rankled. She didn't need anyone looking out for her.

Except tonight she had.

Or had she? After all, it was Devin—or should she say Shock—who had scared the crap out of her.

She glanced down the road at the tough-looking men hanging out at the corner. Their number had grown since the bar had closed. She did *not* want to be roaming around here alone at this hour.

She zipped up her purse. But with no money she couldn't get a cab. The thought crossed her mind to ask Devin if she could borrow some money for a taxi, but she pushed it right out of her mind. She had promised herself long ago that she would never ask for money—or anything else—from Devin.

Anyway, it would all be too complicated. She'd have to arrange to get it back to him, and that would mean contacting him, and she did not want to see him again. Their past relationship was over and should remain in the past. And the way he'd changed . . . she didn't want to get caught up in whatever had changed him. He had his friends and his life, and she had hers. And what was going on in her life was enough to cope with right now without taking on someone else's stuff. Especially when that someone else was Devin, a part of her past she just wanted to forget.

Shock. She had to remember he was Shock now.

"So, will you accept that ride now?" Devin asked.

She glanced up at him, then pursed her lips. "Yes, please."

Shock led her to a big Harley and handed her a black helmet. She pulled it on and stared at the bike.

"Get on," he said.

She frowned, unsure how to do it with a dress on. Before she could pick her strategy, he encircled her waist with his big hands and lifted her onto the bike. Her thighs were spread wide, hugging the black leather seat, and she quickly smoothed her skirt over herself, afraid he'd gotten a glimpse of her pink lace panties. Her cheeks flushed and she realized she was being ridiculous. They were both adults . . . and they were just panties.

Devin grabbed a black leather jacket and helmet and

pulled them on, then mounted the bike in front of her. He settled his big body between her legs, the warmth of him against her inner thighs sending her senses reeling.

"Put your arms around me."

"What?"

He glanced over his shoulder. "You have to hold on to me."

"Oh, right. Sorry." She slid her arms around his waist, her hands resting lightly on the leather of his jacket as she tried not to actually make contact with him.

He pressed her hands tight against his stomach. The feel of his hard muscles under her fingertips, even through the warm leather, sent heat fluttering through her.

"You have to actually touch me to hold on. You don't want to fall off the bike and onto your ass, do you?" He grinned. "If that happened, then you'd be flashing those pink panties of yours to the world."

Her cheeks flushed even hotter.

Then the engine started and the bike shot forward. She sucked in a breath and tightened her hold on him, afraid her ass *would* land on the pavement. When he turned onto another road, she rested her head against his back, clinging to him as the bike leaned to the side.

The feel of the supple leather against her cheek, the manly smell of it, filled her with longing.

Back in college, they used to study together, and they'd become friends. Then it became complicated by a growing attraction between them. If things had happened differently—if that incident hadn't happened—then they probably would have gone somewhere with it. Developed a romantic relationship. Become lovers.

But she couldn't. Not after . . .

Her heart clenched. She'd pulled back and she knew he'd never understood, but there was no way she could have told him about it.

Now, as she clung to him, she wondered what had happened to him—whether his situation had changed or he was just defying his family. But there was no denying that he was earthier. And more rugged.

And at the same time totally intimidating with his badass clothes and his biker attitude. Which, she admitted, was a big part of why she was filled with yearning.

She knew him, but she didn't. Which made him a mystery.

But no matter how big and intimidating he was, she knew what was inside, and that he would never hurt her.

They had left the downtown area and now traveled along the quiet highway. She lived on the outskirts in a low-rent building on the bus line. She heard the sound of engines behind them. She glanced back to see other bikers following them. She noticed Devin glancing in his mirror, his expression drawn tight.

He turned on a side road and one of the bikes pulled up alongside them, then another pulled up on their other side. She thought it might be Devin's friends, but there were four in all. Suddenly the bikes pulled ahead, and the two behind them pulled beside them. The bikes slowed and swerved to the right. Devin tried to pull away from them, but they surrounded the bike and forced him off the road.

"What the fuck are you doing?" Devin shouted as he stopped the bike.

But two of the men grabbed his arms and pulled him from the motorcycle, and she felt a third slide his arm around her waist and pull her roughly from the seat and plunk her on the ground.

"So this guy is good enough for you, but not us?"

Her gaze shot to the owner of the voice. It was Crow from the bar. And she now recognized the others, who had pulled off their helmets, as the guys who had been with him at the bar.

It took all three of Crow's men to restrain Devin as Crow grabbed her arm and pulled her off the side of the road. Liv was terrified as he dragged her toward some trees. The others dragged Devin along with them.

Her captor backed her against a tree and leered at her, his tight grasp on her arm biting into her flesh. He grabbed the neckline of her dress and she gasped as he tore it open, revealing her pink lace bra, her breasts swelling from the top. Someone behind her snickered, and she sucked in a breath, terrified, knowing exactly what he intended to do to her.

He pushed her shoulders back, forcing her against the rough tree bark, his dark, weasel-like eyes locked on the swell of her bosom.

Suddenly, she heard a growl and a thud, then a heavy thump. She glanced around just in time to see one man on the ground and Devin's fist connecting with the jaw of the other one. The third man rushed him from behind, but Devin turned and flipped him onto the grass. With all three men on the ground, he kicked the first, who was starting to get up, in the ribs, then stormed in her direction.

"You get your fucking hands off her." Devin's voice was intimidating and dangerous.

Her captor hesitated, then pulled her from the tree and thrust her toward Devin. He caught her before she stumbled to the ground.

"You oughta keep your fucking girlfriend in line," Crow said. "You let her sit around Matey's like that and a guy gets ideas."

Devin set her to the side and strode toward Crow, then pounded his fist so hard into the guy's face that he dropped to the ground. Blood rushed from his nostrils and Liv was pretty sure Devin had broken his nose.

But Devin wasn't done. He grabbed the guy and pulled him to his feet, then hit him again. And kept on hitting him. Aghast, Liv raced forward and grabbed Devin's shoulder, trying to pull him back.

"No, Devin. Don't. He's not worth it."

"Stay out of this," he snapped, pulling his fist back for another blow.

But she wrapped her fingers around his forearm. "Please. Don't do this."

He stared at her, then scowled. But he released the guy, letting him sag to the ground. He was conscious, but barely.

Devin grabbed her arm and pulled her, stumbling, toward the road again.

"Take care of your asshole leader," he grated as he passed the other three men, who had staggered to their feet again.

He pulled his jacket off and threw it around her shoulders. "Put that on and zip it up."

She nodded, sliding her arms into the sleeves, then pulling up the zipper. It was huge on her, but it covered her semi-nakedness.

"Are you okay?" he asked through gritted teeth as they continued walking.

She nodded, not trusting her words. The truth was she was badly shaken.

He lifted her onto the bike, then mounted it himself.

"Liv, don't call me Devin again. My name is Shock. The man called Devin is long gone."

Then he started the engine and the Harley jolted forward before she had a chance to respond.

Shock took Liv to the address she had given him, and pulled up in front of her building. He wasn't expecting such a run-down place. With her great grades at school and her ambition, he was sure Liv would be doing well in her career. Why would she live in such a dump?

He got off the bike and watched her throw her leg over and slip to the ground, catching another glimpse of her feminine lace panties.

She pulled off the helmet, revealing her tousled honey-blonde hair, which now tumbled in soft waves over the shoulders of his leather jacket.

"Thanks for the ride." She toyed with the zipper on the jacket.

"Keep that on. I'll walk you to your place and get it back there." He sure as hell wasn't going to let her walk around in public with her dress torn open.

She hesitated. Fuck, did she think . . . ?

"Hey, you were just attacked by some asshole. You don't really think I'm going to try something, do you?"

She gazed up at him. "No, of course not."

But she didn't sound as sure as he would have liked.

"I'm walking you to your place and I'm going to make sure you're safe and sound." His tone brooked no argument.

She turned and walked toward the apartment building and he followed her. She pushed her key in the door and turned it. They walked past the threadbare couch in the lobby and into the elevator. A few minutes later they stood at her apartment door. She opened it and glanced up at him.

"I'm coming in," he said. "You're not taking that off out here in the hall."

She nodded, then led him inside.

It wasn't much. A tiny studio apartment with a kitchen on one side with a small round table, a pull-out couch—he assumed because of the bed pillow and blanket sitting on top—and two doors. One probably a bathroom and the other a closet.

She walked to a dresser against one wall and grabbed a sweater from a drawer, then turned her back and slipped off the leather jacket. As she pulled on the sweater, he could see the reflection of her pink-lace-clad breasts in the glass door of the TV cabinet. He should look away, but the sight was mesmerizing. His cock twitched. He had wanted this woman with an unprecedented depth of desire for a very long time.

She zipped up the sweater, then turned to him and handed him his jacket. "Thank you."

He took it with a nod. "How about a cup of coffee?"

"It's kind of late."

"Come on. It's Friday night. And we haven't seen each other in six years."

Liv sighed. "Okay. I think I have some decaf."

She didn't really want him to leave. She was still shaken up by what had happened. In fact, she'd love nothing better than for him to climb into bed with her and hold her all night long. She'd feel safe in his arms. Protected. But that was an insane idea. Anyway, there was no way she'd show him that much weakness.

And she also knew that if he stayed the night, they wouldn't just sleep.

She puttered around the kitchenette making coffee, then set two mugs on the round table and they both sat down.

"So, what happened?" she asked. "Why are you riding around with bikers instead of living in New York, running your family business?"

He frowned, then sipped his coffee. "You never did beat around the bush, did you?"

She shrugged. "It's a huge change for you. Of course I'm curious."

"Let's just say my old life chewed me up and spit me out, but it turned out to be a blessing in disguise."

"That's an awfully cryptic answer."

He glanced around her dingy apartment. "And what about you? This isn't exactly what I expected for you. You had your choice of job offers after college. I figured you'd have a great job. A nice house."

"Not a tiny, crappy apartment," she said, trying to keep the sadness out of her voice.

The fact was she did have a well-paying job. And she worked hard. But she'd recently had to sell her beautiful town house and her car to help with her sister's medical bills.

Several months ago, Julia had started getting sick a lot, and then she'd taken ill with pneumonia. She'd wound up in the hospital and just didn't get better. The doctors kept her in the hospital, doing tests, but two months and a pile of bills later they had theories but nothing conclusive.

Not that she'd tell Shock that. She didn't want him feeling sorry for her.

She was doing enough of that herself.

"Liv, I didn't mean to insult you."

She shrugged. "It's okay. I guess things don't always turn out the way you expect."

He drained his cup, then stood up. His huge frame dwarfed her tiny apartment.

"I should get going."

She stood up, wishing he would stay a little longer. But she wouldn't ask.

"Okay. Thanks again for the ride. And for . . . saving me from those guys."

He frowned. "Are you sure you're okay? I could stay if you want."

"No," she answered too quickly. "It's okay."

"Liv—"

"I'm fine. You don't have to worry about me."

"I'm not worried, but you must still be shaken by what happened."

"I can take care of myself," she said. That was her mantra.

He rested his hand on her shoulder. His gentle touch sent warmth humming through her, and not just a comforting warmth. Her insides heated with that familiar yearning that threw her so off balance when she was around him.

"I know you can."

"Do you?" She stared at him. "Because it didn't sound that way earlier when you said I have no common sense. And come to think of it, you always used to lecture me back in college, too."

He squeezed her shoulder. "So I was a little harsh. I was worried about you, that's all."

"Well, don't be." But her annoyance faded as she saw the warmth in his eyes. Things might have changed, but there was still something between them. There always had been, even though they'd never taken their relationship beyond friendship.

But now, as she stared up at him, the heat of the potent attraction that had always pulsed between them flared to life.

He must have felt it, too, because he slowly lowered his head and she knew she should flee. He was going to kiss her and that kiss would devastate her senses. She knew it. He knew it.

But she was frozen to the spot. Longing for what was about to happen.

His lips brushed hers, and electricity flashed through her. His arms came around her and he drew her gently to his body. He deepened the kiss, singeing her senses. Sending her heart pounding like a kettledrum.

She melted against him and allowed his tongue to glide into her mouth, curling her own around his. She drew in a deep breath, giving herself over to the moment, allowing this experience that she'd yearned for over so many years to completely envelop her.

Then she felt his hand glide up her side and heard the zipper of her sweater as he pulled it down. His hand slid inside and cupped her lace-clad breast.

She gasped and pushed against his shoulder.

He cursed under his breath, then pulled back.

Her dress, gaping open, covered nothing, so she quickly pulled up the zipper of her sweater.

"Fuck, I'm sorry. I shouldn't have done that." He straightened. "I'm going now." Then he turned and strode to the door. He pulled it open and turned to her. "Just promise me you won't go hanging around that bar late at night on your own again."

"Of course," she mumbled, not having the energy to say anything more.

He nodded, then shut the door behind him.

Shock pushed open the door of the building and strode into the night. Fuck, what was wrong with him? That wasn't him.

True, when he'd first suggested driving Liv home, he'd seen it as an opportunity to finally get into her pants. He'd longed to sample her luscious body ever since college, but she'd drawn a definite line in the sand. Despite her own

obvious attraction to him, she'd never allowed their relationship to move past friendship. Now that he'd found her
again, he'd intended to change that. A quick one-nighter
with her should put those old cravings to bed once and
for all.

But when those guys attacked her this evening . . .
fuck, he wasn't going to do something after that. Once she
was in his arms, though, all thought fled his brain and his
throbbing cock had taken control.

She threw him off balance, and he hated that.

Well, there was no reason for him to see her again, so
this was over. And just as well.

He climbed on his bike and took off into the night.

The next morning, Liv hung up the phone, her heart aching. Her sister had taken a turn for the worse. The doctor
told her that they'd found an abdominal aortic aneurysm,
which would kill her if they didn't remove it quickly. Un-
fortunately, because they had determined that Julia had a
fairly rare form of vasculitis, a specialist would need to be
brought in. That meant the surgery would be very expensive and her insurance would cover only a portion of it.

But Liv was already tapped out. She'd sold the town
house and her car, and used up her savings to help Julia.
Julia hadn't asked her to—in fact, she had insisted that Liv
not do it—but Liv couldn't just watch her sister die without doing everything she could to help.

If only Julia's no-good husband, who'd up and left her
six months ago, would help out.

Liv picked up the phone and dialed.

"Yeah," Carl's voice said impatiently on the phone.

"Carl, it's Liv. You stood me up yesterday."

"Yeah, I got held up at work."

"We were supposed to meet at midnight."

"Liv, I work as a bouncer. There was an incident and they needed me to stay past my shift. Nothing I could do."

"You could have called."

"Yeah, sorry."

"Look, I really need to talk to you. It's urgent."

"Okay, tonight. Same time and place."

The thought of going back to Matey's Bar at all, let alone on her own, sent her heart pounding.

"Let's pick somewhere else," she said.

"It'll be fine, Liv."

"It's just . . . there were some guys there . . . They might be there again tonight."

"Fine, if you're nervous, meet me at Burt's, the bar I work at. It's just down the street."

"But—"

"Look, those are your choices. Take it or leave it," he said with finality.

She scowled. "Fine. I'll meet you at Burt's."

She hung up the phone, not looking forward to this evening.

Liv walked inside Burt's and glanced around. The décor was basically Western, like an old-style saloon. Burt's seemed to have a rougher crowd than they did at Matey's Bar, and several unsavory-looking men around the place stared at her. Her skin began to crawl and she had an overwhelming urge to turn around and bolt out of here, but that would just leave her on the street again at midnight. The bus had dropped her off just outside the bar, but it was gone by now, and after last night's adventure, she didn't want to chance waiting for the next one to arrive.

She walked to the bar, hoping to ask the bartender where Carl was.

A waitress stopped by the table and asked if Shock and the others wanted another beer. Rip and Steele were back at the house with their women, just like last night, but Dom, Magic, and Wild Card were with him.

"I'm done," Shock said. He glanced around and Magic shrugged. The others nodded.

The waitress left and Shock sipped his beer, then sat back in his chair. He was getting tired of this whole scene. Rip and Steele had the right idea. Spend the evening pleasuring their women. Maybe, if they went home now, the ladies would like a little extra fun.

He sure could fucking use it.

"Hey, isn't that your girlfriend from last night?" Dom asked.

Shock glanced in the direction Dom was looking. Sure enough, Liv was walking toward the bar. Fuck, did the woman have no sense at all? After what happened last night, he honestly thought she'd stay away from this area.

Men were watching her sweet denim-clad ass as she walked, and annoyance bubbled up inside him. As she approached the bar, a big guy walked right up to her and put his hand on her shoulder. Shock started to get to his feet, ready to spring into action if the guy tried anything, but when she saw the man, a look of relief crossed her face and she followed him to a table.

Was this the guy she'd intended to meet last night?

He watched them as they sat at a corner table talking intently.

"You want to leave?" Magic asked, his glass empty in front of him.

"Give it a minute," Shock said.

The discussion between Liv and her friend seemed to be heated, judging from the guy's tight expression and the look of anxiety on Liv's face. The guy leaned in close, his eyes blazing, and Liv flared right back at him. A moment later, the guy pounded on the table, then stood up and strode out the door.

Liv watched Carl stalk off, anger still blazing through her. How could he be so callous? He was totally unwilling to help.

She knew he was barely making ends meet himself, so it wasn't as if he could do that much, but she'd hoped he could do something. And, of course, it didn't help that Julia had made her swear not to tell him anything about her illness. So all Liv had been able to do was tell Carl that Julia was having some financial problems and needed his help.

She felt so alone. She knew she was looking for a miracle, but that was what it would take to save her sister. A miracle.

"Hey, sweet cakes, I see your boyfriend ran out on you."

She glanced up to see a slightly drunk man grinning at her.

"I could give you a ride home . . . or anywhere else you'd like to go, if you know what I mean."

Oh, she knew what he meant all right. And she also realized that Carl had abandoned her here, all alone, putting her in exactly the same position as she had been last night. But this time she didn't have Shock to come to her rescue.

"No, thank you."

She wondered if she should use her last twenty dollars to call a cab. Payday was next week, and she could stretch the last of her food until then.

She was about to reach for her phone when the guy plunked down on the chair beside her and rested his hand on her arm. When she tried to pull it away, he grasped it. "Come on, honey. I promise to show you a real good time, if you know what I mean."

She tried to pull her hand away again, but he just tightened his grip and panic welled inside her.

"The lady said no."

She swung her head around to see Shock standing there, tall and intimidating, staring at the guy.

"What's it to you?" the man holding her arm said.

"Remove your hand from the lady or I'll remove it from your arm," Shock threatened through gritted teeth.

His three friends from last night—Magic, Dom, and Wild Card—stood behind him.

She felt the man's fingers loosen, then he released her and held up his hands.

"All right. Whatever." He stood up and walked to the bar.

Then Shock's hand clamped around her wrist and he dragged her to her feet.

"What the hell are you doing back here?" he demanded as he marched her out of the bar.

Her lips pinched together as she gave him a sidelong glance, trying desperately to keep up with his long-legged stride. He slowed down a little.

She welcomed the freshness of the night air filling her lungs, after the stale smell of the bar. Shock's friends gave them a little distance while Shock took her aside.

She drew her arm from his grasp. Although her natural impulse was to tell him to mind his own business, she just couldn't find the energy.

"I wasn't here alone" was all she could manage, remembering her promise from last night.

"I noticed. Who was that guy?"

"That was Carl." She didn't explain any further.

"You shouldn't date a jerk like that who'll leave you alone in a place like this."

"I'm not dating him."

Shock frowned. "So what did you intend to do once he stormed off and left you all alone?"

She let out a deep sigh and gazed at him. "To tell you the truth, I was going to call a cab."

He nodded. At least she was being sensible, but after last night . . .

"Give me your phone," he said.

"Why?" she asked.

"So I can put in my number, and the next time you need a ride, you can call. We'll be in town for another couple of weeks."

She handed him her phone, and after he'd added the number, he handed it back to her. She gripped his hand and didn't let go.

"Could we go somewhere and talk?"

Her touch sent wild tremors through him. Fuck, he hated how he felt out of control around her. But he was sure she felt it, too. Maybe she wanted him as much as he wanted her.

Could that be what this was all about?

He gazed at her speculatively. "Like your apartment?"

"No," she said too quickly. "That's not . . . I was thinking we could get a coffee somewhere."

He drew her closer, heat thrumming through him. "I bet you have coffee back at your place."

God, he wanted her. His cock had been in a constant state of arousal since he'd first spied her in the bar yesterday, and since that kiss . . . God, he had to get ahold of himself.

"There's a diner a few blocks from here that'll be quiet," she said. "And it's out of this rough neighborhood."

"All right." Shock turned and started walking, Liv trailing after him. "I'll see you guys later," he said to the others.

His bike was just around the corner.

He handed her a helmet, then mounted the bike. She

climbed on behind him and placed her arms around his waist, then leaned close to him.

His groin tightened and his cock bounced to attention. Fuck, what he wouldn't do to feel her soft hand glide over his hard flesh. To feel it wrap around him and . . .

He started the engine and tore forward, pushing aside the destructive urges. There was nothing between the two of them but old memories. Frustrating memories of him wanting her with a hunger he'd never felt since.

And her rejecting him.

Shock opened the door of the diner and waited for Liv to go in ahead of him. She led the way to a table by the window and they sat down and ordered two coffees.

The waitress brought the coffee right away and Liv wrapped her hands around the warm mug, her fingers suddenly cold. A frigid cold that filled every part of her.

She had decided to ask Shock for his help, but she didn't know how to start. And, gazing at him now in his rough clothes and leather jacket, she wondered if maybe he wasn't living this way by choice.

"So this really is a change for you," she said. "The way you dress. The way you live."

"You're wondering if I lost everything."

The statement jarred her. "No, not at all." Actually she would never have thought that. His family was so wealthy, and Shock was so savvy and intelligent, the thought of him losing everything made no sense to her. "I just assumed you were taking a break."

He shrugged. "Well, in fact, I did lose everything."

He sipped his coffee. "It turned out that my father and brother were embezzling money from the family company. The shareholders didn't want the company to lose its value, so they quietly offered a deal that they wouldn't prosecute if we gave up our family shares and walked away."

"Oh, my God. That's terrible. Why would they do such a thing?"

"I can't begin to explain it. It seems the two of them made some bad personal investments, then got into some pretty heavy gambling and kept falling further and further in debt."

"So you lost your part in the business, too?"

"That's right. The board didn't want anything to do with anyone in my family."

"I'm so sorry. I can't imagine how difficult it was for you to be so betrayed by your family. And abandoned."

Shock nodded. "I haven't spoken to any of them since—my father, my brother, or any of the execs I'd once considered friends. It's amazing how money can destroy relationships."

Liv could see the pain in his eyes and wondered if he had lost a woman, too.

But as much as she felt sympathy for Shock, she also felt her last hope spiraling away. If Shock didn't have any money, then he couldn't be her savior after all.

"So now you're broke."

"No, I *was* broke. After I was ousted from the company my great-grandfather built, I took all the experience I'd gathered over the years and created my own company. It took a few years, but after a few gaming investments took off, the company skyrocketed in value and I made back everything I lost and more."

"Wow, that's quite an accomplishment. Building from the ground up. Your great-grandfather would be very proud."

He shrugged. "I suppose."

"But now you ride with a gang of bikers. What happened to your company? Did you sell it?"

"I still own it, but I leave the daily management of the company to some of the brightest young minds in the business world. After everything that happened in the past, I prefer to manage from a distance."

"That makes sense," she said.

She sipped her coffee. Silence hung between them as she tried to build up the courage to ask him for help.

Shock watched her as she sat across from him. He was pleased that she'd asked him to join her for coffee, and at how interested she was in his life and what had happened to him over the years since they'd parted. Maybe this would be the first step to them rekindling their friendship, and maybe this time, it might develop into more than that.

But he was concerned that she was growing nervous.

Something was wrong. In fact, he'd sensed it earlier. When he'd demanded to know why she'd been in the bar, she'd barely protested, just given him a terse, uninformative explanation. That wasn't like her.

Now she seemed drained.

Sad.

He narrowed his eyes. "What's wrong, Liv?"

She tilted her face up and gazed at him, and his chest compressed at the glimmer of unshed tears in her eyes.

Fuck, had that guy she'd met with at the bar broken up with her? Was she in love with him, and he'd cold-heartedly ditched her?

"I . . ." She blinked quickly, he was sure to stop tears from escaping, then frowned, looking totally forlorn.

"I have a problem and . . ." She sucked in a breath and gazed at him uncertainly. "I could use your help."

"What is it?" It tore at his heart to see her looking so vulnerable.

"I promised myself I'd never do this. That I'd never, ever—"

Her voice broke and a tear welled in her eye. She dashed it away, clearly hoping that he hadn't noticed.

His chest compressed and he took her hands and cradled them in his.

"Just tell me."

"I . . ." She shook her head and gazed down at her cup. "I need money."

He stiffened.

"I see." So that was what this was all about? She wanted money from him? He drew his hands away. And he'd thought . . . Fuck, he'd thought he finally had a shot with her. That she actually cared about him and was trying to make a real connection.

But that was all a lie. She'd just been making small talk, listening to his story as a way of leading up to making her request.

She wanted money from him. That was all.

"Why do you need it?" he asked, not really caring.

She gazed at him, looking totally miserable. "Does it matter?"

He leaned back in his chair and crossed his arms. "I guess not."

His jaw clenched as he stared at her. He couldn't believe she was asking him for money.

And she wouldn't even tell him why she wanted it. Did she just want to get out of that dump of an apartment and needed the down payment for a house? But he didn't think she'd ask for such a big favor—especially from him—for something like that. He knew it would take a lot for her to allow herself to be so indebted to him.

If he thought she had a gambling or drug problem, he wouldn't even consider it, but he was sure that wasn't it. On the other hand, she might borrow it to help someone else out. She wouldn't want to tell him if it was to help out a guy. Maybe that jackass he'd seen her with earlier.

"It might take me some time to pay you back." She toyed with the spoon lying on the table. "But we can agree to a monthly sum and I'll pay it on time every month—I promise."

He raised an eyebrow. "It'll take time because I take it you need a lot of money."

She glanced at him, then stared back at her coffee and nodded.

"How much?" he demanded.

"Fifty thousand," she said hesitantly.

The amount surprised him, but he showed nothing in his expression. Not that he cared about fifty grand. But from her perspective—from anyone's, really—that was a huge loan. Especially based on a friendship in college. A friendship he'd wanted to be so much more, but she'd never allowed.

He remembered when he'd known her in college. At first they'd just been study partners, but as he'd gotten to know her, he'd started to fall for her. There were so many things about her he loved. The way her eyes glittered when she smiled, her quick and agile mind, her melodic laugh, and the sweetness of her nature. He also admired how close she was to her family. She'd lost her parents a few years earlier to a car accident, but the way she'd talked about the times she and her sister and parents had spent together had warmed his heart. Especially since he'd always wanted that with his own family.

The more time they'd spent together, the more he'd known he wanted a real relationship with her.

He remembered the moment he'd let her know how he felt. They'd walked to the courtyard outside the library, overlooking a small pond, and a duck had waddled by, followed by a trail of ducklings. Liv's eyes had lit up when she'd seen them and a small smile had curved her lips. At that moment, he had been so taken by the breathtaking image, he'd leaned in and kissed her.

A moment he had forever regretted.

When he'd released her lips, instead of her looking up at him with a warm smile, she'd averted her gaze and fumbled with her book bag. When he pressed on and asked her out on a date, her eyes had widened and she'd almost seemed panicked, mumbling something about having too heavy a course load to start a relationship and wanting to just be friends, then had practically fled, claiming to have forgotten an appointment. At that moment, he'd realized he hadn't really expected her to say no. Not because of over-confidence on his part, but because he'd thought they'd developed a real connection. When she wouldn't even give him a chance, he'd felt crushed. Her rejection had hurt more than he'd thought possible.

He picked up his coffee and gulped down the rest, which tasted sour in his mouth, then stood up.

"I'll have to think about it." He dropped some bills on the table and strode to the door.

She followed him into the night. As he mounted the bike, she glanced at him, clearly uncertain about whether he was going to give her a ride home.

"Get on the bike," he said curtly.

She climbed on behind him and wrapped her arms around his waist. Her softness pressed against his back sent his hormones surging, and that annoyed him. He lurched the bike forward and raced along the open road, going way too fast. When they got to the highway, he tore along the road, hoping the wind whipping against his face would clear his mind.

But it didn't. When he pulled in front of her building, he was still in turmoil.

She got off the bike and handed him the helmet, then hesitated.

"You said you'd think about it. So, you'll let me know?"

She seemed genuinely worried that he would say no. And there was a very real possibility of that.

Damn it. Anger surged through him. He wanted her to want *him*, but all she wanted was his money.

He got off the bike and walked toward her. Why the fuck shouldn't he get what he wanted, too? As he stepped closer, his gaze raked over her body, the sexy curves accentuated by her tight-fitting jeans and clingy shirt. He wrapped his arm around her waist and pulled her against him.

"So tell me, if I loan you the money, what will you do for me?"

Her big, sky-blue eyes widened. "What do you mean?"

He tugged her closer and captured her mouth, tasting the sweetness of her lips. Her body, so soft against him, so incredibly warm and inviting, drove him crazy. He'd wanted her for so long. Yearned for her.

And she melted against him. Her mouth responded to his, her soft breasts cushioned tightly against his chest. He nudged his tongue between her lips and, God help him, she opened for him, welcoming him inside. His cock ached for her. He wanted to feel her naked skin under his hands.

Without ending the blazing kiss, he pulled his jacket open and tugged her even closer, feeling her nipples blossom against him, so hard that he felt them even through the fabric of her top and bra.

He pushed his hand between their bodies and under her shirt, then cupped her ripe, round breast.

She sucked in a breath and pulled away her sweet, warm lips. "No."

He barely heard her protest, the feel of her soft flesh

in his hand consuming him, but then she pushed against his chest.

"No," she said with more strength.

He gazed down at her and saw, shock and . . . fuck, was that hurt in her eyes?

He released her and stepped back.

What the hell had come over him? This was not the kind of man he wanted to be. Arrogant. Controlling. Demanding whatever he wanted and intimidating people to get it.

That was one of the reasons he'd abandoned his wealthy lifestyle even after making all his money back. He'd never been like that by nature, but he'd seen it in his family and former associates. Seen what money could do to people.

He'd gotten out. And changed. But now . . . with her. Why the fuck did she bring out the worst in him?

He strode to his bike.

"Devin? I mean, Shock?"

He turned and glared at her.

"I . . . uh . . ."

"You'll have my answer tomorrow."

He climbed on his bike and pulled on his helmet.

"And, Liv. Don't come looking for me. I'll find you."

Liv watched Shock race off on his bike, her hands shaking, then she opened the door to her apartment building and got on the elevator. As soon as the doors closed, she slumped back against the wall. The elevator moved upward, counting off the floors.

She couldn't shake the memory of his hard body pressed the length of hers. Of his hot mouth moving on hers. She brushed her fingertips over her lips, still swollen and warm from his passionate kiss.

And the feel of his big, masculine hand cupped around her breast. Her nipples still ached with need. She'd pushed him away because it had been too sudden. Too much.

The doors opened and she walked down the hall to her apartment, then opened the door.

She shouldn't lie to herself. She'd pushed him away because she was afraid. She'd always wanted Shock—even back in college. What happened to her back then still affected her profoundly. But even if that weren't true, she feared what would have been unleashed in her if she'd allowed him to continue. If she and Shock had wound up here in her apartment, she might have gotten past her fear, letting him take her on the couch or maybe even against the wall.

That thought frightened her, for more reasons than she wanted to admit.

Shock tossed another rock across the water, watching it skip across the sunlit surface, then disappear.

"What are you doing?" Raven sat down beside him on the grass along the shore of the lake and clasped her arms around her knees. Her long, black hair cascaded over her shoulders as she leaned forward, watching him.

Raven was Rip's woman and had joined the group about a year ago. She was the first woman to join the crew, and she'd fit right in. She was fun and supportive, and she loved sharing her body with all of them.

A few months later, Wild Card had wound up accidentally kidnapping another woman, Tempest, then they were all pursued by the police. In the end, they had saved Tempest from an abusive ex-boyfriend and their leader, Steele, had fallen in love with her. Now the two women rode with them and had sex with all of them, making for quite a friendly, intimate group.

He leaned back against the tree behind him. "Thinking," he said in answer to her question.

"Yeah? You've been doing a lot of that lately."

He picked up another stone, a nice, flat, smooth one, and flicked it sideways over the water's surface. This one skipped five times.

"Have I?" he asked.

She leaned against him. "Yeah. Most of the time you seem a million miles away. Anything to do with a woman?"

"Why do you ask that?"

"Well, Wild Card told me about the woman you've seen in town. Two nights in a row."

"Yeah? And what did he tell you about her?"

"Just that you knew each other in college, that you lectured the poor girl on hanging out alone in rough bars in the middle of the night, then you drove her home. Both nights."

"Are you going to tell me that's not good advice? Did you know she got attacked the first night?"

Raven's smile disappeared. "No. What happened? Is she okay?"

He picked up another stone, rubbing his thumb over the warm, flat surface.

"Yeah, she's fine. I was with her. Some jerks tried to pick her up in the bar, then when I drove her home, they forced us off the road."

Raven gazed at him, her expression serious. "Did they hurt her?"

He compressed his lips. "There was no fucking way I'd let them hurt her."

Her smile returned. "So you took on the lot of them and then carried your lady off into the night."

"Sure, something like that."

She leaned close and stroked her finger over his lower lip. "I thought your lip looked a bit fatter than usual." Her eyes glittered. "I'd assumed that was from kissing."

The light brush of her fingers on his lips reminded him of Liv's lips on his. Of that devastating kiss they'd shared, and need rose in him.

He wrapped his hands around her waist. "Fuck, Rave, it's been quite a while."

Her round, perfect breasts, showcased in the fitted black T-shirt she wore, beckoned to him.

Her eyebrows arched. "You mean your lady didn't reward you?"

"We don't have that kind of relationship." Then he pulled her against his body and found her lips, plundering them with passion.

Her tongue matched his stroke for stroke, and when he drew back, her eyes gleamed.

"Oh, wow. That kiss tells me that maybe you should rethink your relationship with the woman."

Shock took her lips again.

Raven flattened her hand on his chest and pressed him back. "Shock, sweetie, you know I love you and that Rip doesn't mind sharing me, but if he saw you kissing me like that . . ." She shook her head.

Damn, even Raven was turning him down.

But then he felt his zipper glide down. He glanced at her and she giggled when she saw his expression.

"You didn't think I was going to leave you all frustrated, did you?"

She reached inside his jeans and wrapped her fingers around his aching cock.

Aching because he couldn't stop thinking about Liv. And somehow that didn't feel right.

She stroked him and blood pulsed through him.

"Rave, you know, it doesn't seem fair to you—"

She squeezed him, stopping his words. "What? That you're going to be thinking of her?"

She leaned down and licked the base of his shaft. "Don't worry about that. When I'm doing this to you"—she licked him again, from base to tip, sending his hormones fluttering—"you can think of whoever you want."

Then she wrapped her mouth around his tip and sucked. He groaned, then reached out and stroked her hair, gliding his fingers through the silky strands. He leaned back against the tree and imagined it was Liv's long, honey-blonde hair curled around his fingers. That it was her mouth gliding down on him, taking him deep.

Her soft hands that fondled his balls. Her that sucked him.

God, he was so revved up, his yearning so powerful,

that he already felt it . . . that heat deep within him that concentrated in his belly, then burned hotly as it spread through his entire body.

It was heaven feeling Liv's lips around him. Feeling her hands on him. Feeling her touching him intimately. Pleasuring him.

She squeezed her hand around his shaft, then sucked harder.

"Oh, God," he groaned as his balls tightened, then pleasure jolted through him as his cock pulsed, releasing steaming liquid into her mouth.

She continued to suck him, drawing every last drop from his body.

He caressed her hair, drawing it back from her face, then opened his eyes.

Raven stared at him with her big, green eyes.

It wasn't Liv. He'd known that, but his heart ached a little.

But he drew Raven in for a kiss.

"Thanks, Rave."

She smiled and stroked his whisker-roughened cheek with her soft hand.

"Hey, that was the fantasy. Now I think you should go after the real thing."

Liv tossed and turned all night, both regretting having asked Shock to loan her money and hoping that he would be Julia's savior. She spent the day puttering around the apartment, including spending a futile hour trying to clean the rust stains off the yellowed shower tiles in the bathroom.

Late in the afternoon, she got a text from Shock telling her he'd pick her up in fifteen minutes. He had an answer for her.

She waited for him at the front of the building. He said nothing when he arrived, just gestured for her to get on the back of the bike. She climbed aboard and he drove to the highway, then let out the throttle. The wind rushed against her face as she clung to him.

Finally, rather than taking her to a diner to talk, he turned onto a side road, then pulled off on a country lane and followed a smaller dirt path to a grassy field by one of the small lakes in the area.

"Nice view," she said as she dismounted and glanced around.

He glanced over the water. "I like the outdoors. Better than a stuffy diner, don't you think?"

She nodded. She didn't care where he told her his decision, as long as it was the right one.

"So you have an answer for me?" she asked.

He nodded curtly. "I do." His steely gaze pierced through her. "But I don't think you're going to like it."

Liv's stomach clenched. "Oh." Her heart sank. "I take it that you won't loan me the money, then."

"I didn't say that."

Liv stared at him in confusion. "I don't understand."

"I've decided I will lend you the money . . . but there's a condition."

"What is it?"

He moved close to her and dragged her into his arms, driving his tongue into her mouth so deeply that she almost choked in panic. She pressed her hands flat against his chest and pushed halfheartedly, but he tightened his muscular arms around her, pulling her tight against his hard body. Her arms grew limp as she became mesmerized by the heat of him and his mouth ravaging hers so thoroughly.

Then he eased up and became more seductive. He stroked her tongue with his while he glided his hand along her back. Remembering their last two encounters, she feared he'd cup her breast again, but he didn't. His hand slid down and pressed on the small of her back, pulling her pelvis tightly against his big body. So tightly that she could feel the ridge of his growing erection.

This time she found the strength to push back, at least a little, then sucked in air.

"You want me to . . ."—she stared into his steely brown eyes—". . . to date you?"

"Sweetheart, it's not a date I want from you." He leaned in closer, his hot breath stirring her hair. His groin pressed against hers, the hard bulge of his erection telling her exactly what he did want.

"I want you naked and moaning," he said, "my hard cock driving into you. I want your hands all over me,"—his gaze dropped to her lips—"your mouth all over me. I want to fuck you so hard, you scream my name at the top of your lungs." The hand on her lower back pulled her tighter against his pelvis, so she could feel exactly how long and hard he was. "And after you do that, and you're lying gasping on the bed, I want to do it all over again."

She stared up at him and gulped, her eyes wide.

"But . . ." She shook her head, his erotic words searing through her. Did he really think she'd repay him with her body? "You know I would pay you back every cent of the loan. With interest."

"Of course you would. But your interest . . . doesn't interest me." His dark, lust-filled eyes captured hers. "This would be a better . . . incentive," he murmured. "To make the arrangement worth my while."

"Surely you don't handle your business deals this way?" She didn't know what she was saying. She was just trying to think of any way to dissuade him from this crazy demand.

"Of course I don't. Because those are *just* business. What you're asking for is a favor based on a personal relationship." His hands stroked her down to her ass, then cupped it and pulled her forward, causing the ridge of his cock to dig deeper into her belly. "So I think it's appropriate to ask for something more personal in the way of incentive."

She began to tremble. "So you're suggesting we spend the night together?"

He laughed harshly. "Sweetheart, for fifty grand, it's going to be a hell of a lot longer than one night." He raised an eyebrow. "And I expect you to be one exceptional fucking lay."

His harsh words were like a slap across the face. Her stomach clenched and she drew in a shaky breath. Could she actually do this?

"If I agree, then you'll loan me the money?"

His eyes narrowed. "That's right."

"Do I have any other options?" She knew asking that didn't put her in a good negotiating position, but what did it matter? He clearly knew what he wanted and she doubted she would be able to quibble about the details.

"No," he said flatly.

Anxiety quivered through her, but she drew her shoulders back and met his gaze, then nodded.

"Good." He released her and suddenly turned all business. "I'll have my lawyers draw up a contract."

Her gaze shot to his face. "You're kidding."

"I never kid about a business deal."

"But you said this was personal."

"I said it's not *just* business. I'm loaning you a shitload of money, so I'll be laying out the terms in writing to ensure we both know exactly what's involved in this deal."

When the brown envelope arrived by courier the next day, Liv signed for it and took it from him, then sat on the couch and stared at it.

Could this really be happening? The terms of a sexual relationship with Shock laid out in a dry, legal document, stating what was expected of her?

She ripped open the flap and pulled out a manila folder with a couple of documents inside. Stark white paper with black words in a sterile typeface. She tried to read the words, but she found the phrasing and the long paragraphs written in legalese daunting. And she couldn't stop thinking about the fact that he'd sat down with a lawyer and laid out the salient points and pertinent details to draw up this contract.

Oh, God, when her gaze scanned over the phrase

"agrees to submit to" and "including, but not confined to, sexual acts," she slammed the folder closed, unable to read any further.

She picked up the phone and dialed the cell number Shock had given her if she needed to contact him.

Shock sat on a rock with his legs stretched out in front of him. Raven and Laurie, who now went by the ride name "Tempest," were swimming in the lake with a couple of the guys. He was pretty sure the skimpy bikinis the girls were wearing would soon disappear, since the sexual banter had shifted up a notch. He watched Raven as she adjusted her strap, which had slipped off her shoulder, then his gaze locked on the single sparkling droplet of water gliding down between her wet breasts.

Fuck, his cock insisted he strip off his clothes right now and dive into the water, but what he wanted was a woman of his own, not to share someone else's. And the woman he wanted was Liv. He wanted to taste her sweet mouth again, to stroke her smooth flesh. And for her to be willing and pliable in his arms.

Or fighting and struggling, if that was the way she liked it. And part of him hoped she did. At least sometimes.

"Hey, you can do more than look, you know," Rip said as he sat down on a fallen tree trunk beside him.

"Why aren't you out there with Raven?" Shock asked.

"What, and spoil her fun? She usually likes me involved in her group play, but occasionally she likes to be with the guys solo."

But Rip was clearly turned on. Shock couldn't help but notice Rip's jeans stretched taut over a thickening erection.

Shock glanced at Tempest, Steele's woman, standing knee-deep in the water, her gorgeous body on display.

"There are other options," Shock said.

There was a light buzzing sound, and Rip reached into his pocket and pulled out a cell phone. It was the only one they had. As a group, they'd elected to have limited interaction with the outside world.

"Yeah," Rip said, gazing distractedly at Tempest. "Just a sec." Rip held out the phone to Shock. "It's for you."

Shock took the phone. "Yeah, Shock here."

He watched Rip head toward the water, shedding his clothes as he went.

"Hi, it's Olivia."

He arched an eyebrow. "So formal, Liv? I take it you received the contract."

"Yes, I did."

"Is there a problem?" he asked, sensing it in her tight voice. He wasn't really surprised. Seeing everything all laid out in black and white was bound to shake her up.

"I'm not really comfortable with the contract."

"So you want to cancel the whole thing?"

"No," she answered quickly. "It's not that. It's just . . . well, I'm not a lawyer and . . . it's a little overwhelming."

"Okay, I'll come over and discuss it with you in person. I'll be there in a half hour."

When he arrived at the front door of her building, she buzzed him up. A few moments later, he knocked on her apartment door.

She opened it, then stepped aside to let him in. She sat on the couch, her head hanging as if she'd lost her best friend.

"So what's the problem?"

"I've taken a closer look at it since I called you." She raised her head and glared at him. "There's a whole list of sexual things you've listed that I have to do, and I'm not comfortable with that."

"Liv, that's a standard sexual contract. Many couples draft this kind of thing before they enter into a relationship these days. In the short-term relationship we're about to enter, I thought it was especially important to make sure our terms are clear."

"But you've ticked off every sexual act," she cried in exasperation.

"True. What's your point?" Of course, he was going to give her a contract that gave him exactly what he wanted. One that was designed to give him the most freedom to explore a wild, sexual adventure with her.

She stared at him in shock. "There are some I just . . . *can't.*"

He was surprised. Liv always seemed to act in such a rash and fearless manner, he didn't think there'd be anything on that list she would find objectionable. She might not have done them all, but he figured she'd be game to give them a try. The point of putting them on the list was to get her thinking wild and incredibly erotic thoughts. Pushing the limits beyond anything she'd done before.

"Like what?" he asked.

She bit her lip and gazed down at the contract. It seemed painful for her to scan the page of words.

"Well, this thing called fisting. I don't know what that is, but I don't like the sound of it."

He lifted his hand and pinched his fingers together.

"Fisting is where I make a fist, or just press my fingers together like this, and push my whole hand—"

"No," she blurted. "Don't tell me. I definitely don't want to do that."

"Okay. What else?"

"There are things about . . ." She frowned and gazed at him helplessly. "Uh . . . anal stuff." Her cheeks had darkened to a deep rose. "And handcuffs, gags . . . sex toys."

At his silence, she continued. "And it even says that . . . oh, God, that you can tell me to have sex with other men. And *watch*."

Her emphasis on the last word was almost comical. Was she really so staid sexually? Sure, maybe she drew the line at more than one lover, but no sex toys? Nothing anal? He'd really thought she was more adventurous than that.

"Come on, Liv. Are you saying you wouldn't like several hot bikers touching you . . . caressing you?"

Her eyes widened. "Several? I assumed you meant one. At least, at a time."

"Is that your boundary? Just one at a time?"

"No! I have no boundary." At his smile, she stuttered, "I mean, I've never thought about it. I don't know where my boundary is."

"Really? You've never fantasized about being made love to by several men at once?"

Her cheeks flushed even darker.

"The clause stays in," he said.

She bit her lip, obviously wanting to argue.

"Look, Liv, I'm not saying we'll do all of these things, but I want you to at least be open to them."

"This is a contract. If I sign it, I have to do them."

"If I tell you to."

"Yes." She sounded doubtful.

"Look, I'm not going to demand that you do each and every thing on that list whether you want to or not."

In fact, he wouldn't push any of them. Nothing in the sexual contract was enforceable by law, and in fact he wouldn't do anything she clearly didn't want to do. He just wanted to get her thinking about pushing beyond her limits.

"I tell you what," he said. "You go through and mark off the things you're willing to do and we'll see what compromise we can come up with."

She pursed her lips. "Okay."

She fetched a red pen and started going through the list. Each item had a place to indicate if Liv was willing to receive the action, to perform the action, and if there were limitations, and what those limitations were.

He watched her while she gazed at the list and crossed off item after item. "Vaginal fisting" and "anal fisting." Not surprising.

"Performing sex with another partner or partners." "Anal intercourse."

When she lowered the pen to cross out "fellatio," he protested. "Really, Liv?"

She glanced up at him, her cheeks now a deep crimson. She pursed her lips and shifted the pen, leaving the item unmarked. Then she crossed out "swallowing semen." *Damn.*

When she was finished, she handed him the sexual contract, which was an addendum to the contract itself.

He glanced over the paper and realized she'd vetoed everything but "kissing," "vaginal intercourse," and "fellatio," and the latter only because he'd called her on it. She hadn't even agreed to "cunnilingus."

He glanced at her. "Let me use your computer and I'll print out a new agreement."

She stood up and retrieved a laptop from a shelf and set it on the table. He sat down and pulled up the copy of the agreement from the e-mail his lawyer had sent him, then modified it. He sent it to the printer and a few seconds later a little printer on her bookshelf chugged out the page.

Liv picked it up and scanned it. She frowned as she walked to the table.

"You didn't make any of my changes," she protested.

"I took out the fisting. And a few of the toys." Mostly medical devices, which he wasn't interested in anyway, and would clearly freak her out.

She stared at the list. "So, basically, because I'm borrowing money from you, I'm your sex slave?"

"I'm not going to force you to do anything you don't want to do. I just want you to be open to trying new things." He took the paper from her. "And I want you to trust me."

She scowled. "There's nothing on this list I want to do with you."

Annoyance buzzed through him.

"Sign the contract, Liv. Then my lawyers will release the money into your bank account this afternoon."

She glared at him, then picked up a pen and sat down

with the contract in front of her. She put the pen to paper, then hesitated.

"Wait. There's one more thing," she said.

"I'm listening."

"The contract states that I'm to be . . . uh . . . with you for one month. Does that mean you'll be coming over here every day? Or I'll be going wherever you live? You know, I work pretty long hours at work, so it's more practical if we see each other only on weekends."

"No."

"Well, as I said, we can meet in the evenings, but—"

"That won't work." He flipped through the contract and frowned. "I'm sorry, there seems to have been an oversight." He glanced at her. "There was supposed to be a section in the contract about the fact you will be available to me twenty-four hours a day. I'll have to have an addendum added." He glanced at her. "Not only will you not be going to work, but you'll be riding with me. We're only staying here another couple of days, then we hit the road. Your month with me starts in three days."

"But I can't do that. That's too short notice to get the time off and I couldn't get a whole month anyway."

"It's not a problem."

"It *is* a problem. I'll lose my job."

"No, you won't. I've arranged to hire you as a consultant from your company. All they know is that you'll be working for my company for one month."

"But I'm not a consultant."

"I know that's not your usual role, but I offered enough money that they accepted. They'll let you know first thing tomorrow and you'll continue to draw your salary for the month."

At the flush starting across her cheeks again, he said, "Don't worry. They have no idea what our real arrangement is."

"So it seems I owe you even more money."

He should have realized she'd take it that way.

"Don't worry about it."

"As we've already established, I really have no choice, do I?"

At that, she picked up the pen and signed the contract.

Liv continued to be angry and embarrassed about the contract and the way Shock was treating her, but she pushed the feelings aside while she dealt with everything she needed to do before she left with him.

Shock had followed through with his promise to move the money to her account immediately, even before she signed the addendum he added about the consulting contract. She arranged for Julia's surgery, which was scheduled within a week. Shock wanted her to start her time with him right away, but she told him she had family business to attend to and she needed some time.

A week after the surgery, to Liv's delight, Julia seemed to be recovering quite nicely. Liv didn't want to leave while Julia was still in the hospital, but Julia insisted Liv head off on her business trip. Since Julia was so weak, her doctor said they were going to keep her in the hospital for at least a month anyway, so Julia suggested that it was better that Liv go while she was still in their care and be back by the time she was ready to go home.

Liv finally acquiesced. Of course, Liv didn't tell her that she was really traveling with a gang of bikers for a month.

She let Shock know that she would like to leave as soon as possible and he informed her that she needed to go out shopping to buy clothing for the trip. He wanted her to fit in with the biker gang he was traveling with, so he sent a personal shopper to pick out clothes for her. It amazed her that the cost of such seemingly casual clothes was so exorbitant.

Shock had personally picked out the jeans she was to wear, and just one pair of those jeans cost more than her most expensive business suit for work. But they fit her perfectly and made her ass look fantastic.

They also had a zipper that traveled the full length of her crotch.

Then there was the lingerie, if items made of leather were actually considered lingerie. Although he had chosen some lace and silk items, too. She wasn't even sure what some of the other things were. Mostly they consisted of leather straps, studs, and chains.

The day before she was to leave, she packed everything up in the backpack he'd also bought for her, then went to visit Julia again, but she didn't stay long because her sister was tired.

Liv then stopped by the facility where her grandmother was staying. Gran was suffering from dementia, and Liv had had to put her there a year ago, as much as it broke her heart to do it. But she just couldn't take care of Gran well enough by herself. She had been dropping by a few times a week, until Julia wound up in the hospital. Since then, Liv's visits to Gran had been sporadic, which left her guilt-ridden. She would do better when she got back, she promised herself.

When Liv got home, she made dinner from the left-overs in the fridge, then busied herself with cleaning out the fridge of perishables, tossing the garbage, and doing last-minute tasks in preparation for her departure.

When she finally climbed into bed, she stared at the ceiling, sleep eluding her.

What was the next month going to be like? What demands would Shock actually make of her?

She pulled the covers closer.

And how would he react when he found out she was virtually a virgin?

In the morning, Liv got up and showered, trying not to think about the adventure she was about to embark on. But despite the anxiety that gripped her about the relationship she was about to enter into with Shock, she was a little thrilled at the idea of having a month off from her usual worry-filled existence.

It would be exciting to ride on the back of Shock's motorcycle and to meet his friends, although that also filled her with trepidation.

As she sat and drank her coffee, her phone bleeped. She checked the text message she'd just received.

Will be there in 20 minutes.

She sighed and finished her coffee, then dressed in a pair of the designer jeans and a T-shirt with glittery skulls and roses. She brushed her long blonde hair, then threw her backpack over her shoulder and headed downstairs.

Shock pulled up in front of her building right on time. His gaze heated as he glanced up and down her body appreciatively. The high heels on her leather boots were spiked and sexy, with metal tips, and the feet were adorned with studs. The boots, along with her jeans, which were tight in all the right places, made her legs look long and her behind look shapely.

She was very conscious of the zipper along the crotch of her pants. It wasn't uncomfortable—the pants were very well designed—but she felt conspicuously sexy in them, as if they were an invitation to him to unzip them and have his way with her.

Which maybe he intended to do.

"Good morning. Had breakfast yet?" he asked.

"No, just some coffee." She hadn't been very hungry, and she'd cleaned out the fridge yesterday, so there hadn't really been anything on hand.

"It's about a ten-hour drive. You need to eat. We'll stop and get something on the way."

He handed her a helmet and she climbed on the bike behind him.

The heat of his body between her legs sent warmth humming through her. He started the engine and she wrapped her arms around his solid body, the leather soft and supple against her hands. Soon they were speeding along the highway.

The wind whipping against her cheeks was exhilarating, and she loved watching the scenery, mostly trees and meadows, flashing by. After about an hour, the lack of sleep got to her and she leaned her head against his back. The scent of leather and warm male filled her nostrils as she closed her eyes and rested.

Time seemed to drift by, then she felt the bike slow and pull off the road.

"Time for breakfast," he said, stopping in front of a diner. "I didn't mean to drive so long. Maybe some food will revive you. I don't want you drifting off to sleep and falling off the bike."

She glanced at her watch and realized they'd been riding for two hours. Her stomach rumbled.

Inside the diner, she glanced at the menu, then ordered an omelet and toast. Shock ordered a huge plate of bacon, sausage, eggs, and pancakes.

"So, where are we going?" she asked.

"We're staying at a country house I own north of here. It's on a lake, with a great view. The others will arrive tomorrow."

"So, it's not just the two of us?"

He smiled. "Would you prefer that?"

She didn't know how to answer. She didn't know how to act around his biker friends, and she was worried about the idea of him wanting to share her with the other men, but being alone with him seemed worse.

"Don't worry. You'll get along fine with the guys. And there are two other women traveling with us. I think you'll like Raven and Tempest."

She just nodded and sipped her coffee. The waitress brought their food.

As they ate, they made small talk about the trip and the weather, then they hit the road again. The day sped by like the miles they put behind them. When they stopped for dinner, they still had another three hours to go.

A couple of hours later, Shock pulled off the road again at a gas station and stopped in front of the gas pump.

"Go inside and grab a couple of bottles of water," he said, "while I fill the tank."

Liv dismounted the bike and walked into the convenience store. A group of three guys lounging around the snack bar glanced her way, eyeing her jeans and black leather jacket, the helmet tucked under her arm. One of them laughed and made a comment about how hot the zipper on the jeans was, and she could see in the security mirror that they were looking at her ass.

She kept walking to the cooler at the back of the store and opened it, then pulled out two bottles of water. She could still feel their gazes on her, though, and it sent a chill through her.

She turned and caught one guy staring at her with a leering smile, then he pushed himself away from the counter he was leaning against and started to walk toward her.

The bell over the door chimed and the guy glanced around to see Shock, who looked particularly intimidating, his leather-jacketed six-foot-five-inch frame filling the doorway as he sent the guy a menacing glare.

The guy turned nonchalantly and began talking to his friends. Shock headed her way.

"Got the water?" He stared at her almost accusingly, as if he thought she'd sent a blatant invitation to the guy.

"Right here." She held up the cold bottles and he took them from her, then walked to the cashier and paid.

They stepped outside into the warm night. He led her to the bike, which he'd parked near a picnic table on the grass. He put his helmet on the wooden surface and sat down, then opened one water bottle and handed it to her. She sat across from him, placing her helmet next to his.

She drank her water, watching him, but he paid no attention to her. Crickets chirped in the background and the occasional car passed by on the road. She shifted on the wooden bench seat, annoyed at the silence hanging between them.

"I didn't do anything to encourage that guy, you know," she finally bit out.

He took a swig of his water and nodded.

She narrowed her eyes. "The way you looked at—"

His sharp gaze pivoted to her, stopping her cold. "I was looking at him, not you." He gulped back the rest of the water. "You can't help it if guys look at you. But no one messes with my woman." He crumpled the empty bottle in his hand. "He was lucky he didn't try to touch you. If he had, he'd be a bloody pile of broken bones by now."

She didn't argue with the "my woman" crack. According to their agreement, for the next month, that was exactly what she was.

A part of her wanted to feel affronted by his possessive behavior, which seemed to imply that he didn't think she could take care of herself. But in truth, she found his possessiveness and protectiveness . . . nice. It made her feel taken care of. Something she hadn't felt in a very long time.

"It doesn't help that you've dressed me in these come-hither jeans."

He chuckled. "Really? 'Come-hither'?"

She stared at him, surprised at his change in demeanor, but then she realized it was pretty funny. "I suppose that did sound like something from an old-fashioned romance novel. Would 'fuck-me' jeans work better for you?"

His grin faded and heat blazed in his eyes. "If you only knew." He stood up. "Ready?"

She took another sip and recapped the half-empty bottle, then handed it to him. He stared hungrily at her lips, then turned and tucked it in the side bag. She tried to ignore the heat crackling between them as she put on her helmet and climbed on the bike.

He pulled on his own helmet. "We still have an hour on the road ahead of us."

And she knew what was at the end of that road. The first time she and Shock would be alone together. In a bed-room.

Would he be tired after the long ride and want to wait, or would he take her right away?

He mounted in front of her. "It's all quiet, forest roads. There won't be much to see."

She wrapped her arms around him, ready for him to start up the engine and take off.

"It could get a bit boring, and I know you wouldn't want me dozing off."

She frowned. What was he getting at?

He took her hand and drew it under his jacket and shirt, then pressed it flat against his sculpted abs. The warm, hot flesh was stretched tight over hard muscles.

"I want you to help keep me awake."

Oh, God, was he kidding? She glanced at the convenience store, but no one was looking their way. All they'd see would be her arms around his waist anyway.

The engine roared to life, then he drove from the parking lot and turned onto the road. She clung to him as he accelerated, one hand still flat on his hard stomach where he'd placed it. Soon they were driving full speed down the dark, deserted road.

After a few moments, he placed his hand on hers and slid it down, over the growing bulge in his pants. He pressed her hand tightly to him, then encouraged her to move it up and down, but the feel of his thick column against her palm was overwhelming. She froze, uncertain what to do. He squeezed her fingers around him, until she was gripping him, then he moved her hand up and down until she continued on her own.

She could feel the outline of his big cock, hard and thick inside his pants. And growing bigger. God, it was impressive. She couldn't imagine that thing inside of her. The thought sent trepidation through her.

And excitement. Her soft insides ached at the thought of him gliding it into her. Her muscles contracted. She thought she heard a groan over the sound of the engine, and he arched forward. It was then she realized she'd squeezed her fingers around him.

Excitement surged through her as she realized the power she had over him. She squeezed him again and stroked him up and down, feeling the outline of his big erection. Longing to unzip his jeans and slip her hand inside.

She wanted to feel his hot flesh. Wanted to feel it burning against her skin.

Could she be so bold?

He twitched against her hand. Hell, he'd probably be thrilled.

She grabbed the tag of his zipper and pulled it down.

Shock felt the zipper on his jeans loosen. Fuck, what was she doing to him?

He'd only expected her to stroke him a few times, maybe a light teasing touch every now and again, but once he'd felt her hand on him, he'd pushed her.

Now she was running with it.

Her delicate hand slid into the opening of his jeans and wrapped around his aching cock, only the thin cotton of his boxers between them.

God, if she kept giving him attention like this, he'd explode all over her hand. And at sixty miles per hour, that wasn't the smartest thing to do. He could handle a bike through almost anything, but a distraction like that . . . he didn't want to put her in danger.

Then her fingers found his naked flesh and he groaned.

One stroke and he was trembling with need.

Another and—

He slammed his hand on hers to stop the movement, then drew it away and zipped up his pants.

He could feel her body tense behind him, then her hands tentatively gripping his waist. Shit, she must feel she didn't know what the hell he wanted.

He took her hand in his and squeezed, then placed it lightly on his cock—his full, close-to-bursting cock. He pressed his hand on top of hers and just held her there, focusing on controlling his raging hard-on.

She got the idea and left her hand there, even after he pulled his away. Occasionally, she would stroke lightly or give him a gentle squeeze. The result was that by the time they arrived at the house, his cock was on a hair trigger.

He pulled up in front of the big country house. Between him and the others in Steele's crew, they had a great network of houses to stay at. Mostly through Shock's connections, since he knew a lot of rich people who had country homes they never used, but some of the other guys knew people with cottages they let them stay at, too. This, however, was Shock's own house.

He pulled the bags from the storage compartment, then grabbed Liv's hand as soon as she dismounted and dragged her toward the door. He was so turned on that he could hardly wait to get her into the bedroom.

He pulled open the front door of the dark, quiet house and led her up the stairs to the master bedroom. Once inside, he closed the door, dropped the bags on the floor, and turned to her, pushing her up against the wall. He claimed her lips, his arms gliding under her jacket and over her back, pulling her tightly to him.

"Fuck, I've waited so long for this," he murmured, then claimed her lips again.

Liv felt overwhelmed as his big body pressed against her, the bulge of his erection hard against her belly. His kiss swamped her senses, sending her head spinning.

Then she felt his hands moving at her waist and realized he was undoing her belt. The zipper of her jeans glided open and he started to push them down with one hand.

Panic welled in her.

His other hand glided over her breast as his tongue plundered her mouth.

She tore her mouth free. "Shock, wait."

His hand stroked the front of her panties, then his fingers glided over the thin fabric covering her crotch.

"Wait for what, baby?" he asked, his voice full of need.

The feel of his fingers on her there sent a wild rush of desire through her, but at the same time it acted like a slap across the face.

"No, please." She pushed against his chest.

He frowned, staring down at her. "What the fuck's wrong?"

"I . . ." She gazed away from his steely brown eyes. "I've never done this before," she admitted.

"Never done what?" he asked in a daze.

"*This*," she hissed in exasperation.

His eyes narrowed. "You're saying you're a virgin?"

"Well, not technically."

He eased back a little. "There's only one technicality. A pretty big one."

At his words, all she could think about was his big cock still pressed tight against her.

"And it either did or didn't happen."

The thought of his cock gliding inside her filled her with panic.

"It did. Once." She bit her lip. "But it wasn't my choice."

His body stiffened against her, then he slowly eased back.

"Are you saying you were raped?" he said in a low, dangerous tone.

She blinked back tears. She'd tried not to think about it. She didn't want to feel the debilitating vulnerability again.

"No. Well, yes."

"Which is it?"

"I fell asleep at a party. At a friend's house. I'd had a bit to drink and went into her spare room. I woke up and . . ." She gulped back a sob, remembering the guy on top of her. Pushing into her.

"Fuck." Shock slid his arms around her and drew her close, then stroked her back. Soothing her.

The guy had been a friend. They'd had classes together in college. Often studied together. He'd give her copies of his notes when she'd missed classes and vice versa. She'd gotten the feeling he was attracted to her, and she'd tried to give him the hint that she didn't feel the same way about him. In fact, she was attracted to Devin—Shock—at the time.

The key was, she had trusted him, and he had betrayed her. She'd never really been able to trust anyone since then.

Shock stroked her hair and she realized she couldn't just feel sorry for herself. She drew back and looked up at him.

"I'm sorry I didn't tell you sooner, but . . . I . . ." She drew in a breath. "It doesn't change what we're doing here. I made a promise to you, and I mean to keep it. I just . . ." She pursed her lips. "If you can just be patient with me at first." She rested her hand on his big, hard chest. "Then I promise, I won't hold back."

He scowled, and she was afraid she'd made him mad. Was he angry because she hadn't confessed her inexperience? He expected her to be sexy and bold. Not some shivering virgin afraid of her own shadow.

Not that that was her. She might be nervous, but she would never quiver from any man.

"Fuck, what kind of monster do you think I am? I'm not going to force you to—"

"No!" she blurted, anger boiling through her. "You are not forcing me. I gave my word and I intend to keep it, and no one—not you or anybody else—is going to stop me from doing that."

She pushed her jeans to the floor and stepped out of them, then, summoning her courage, she pushed down her panties.

"Liv"—Shock said, gazing at her face—"you can't expect me to—"

"To what? Fuck the damaged girl? The one who got raped and now can't function as a normal woman?" Those last words sent chills through her, because, despite her bravado, they were much too close to the truth.

She should have told him about this before, but he might have thought she was just trying to get out of their agreement. No, it was actually because she'd been afraid he would change his mind about the whole thing and not loan her the money she had needed so badly. Clearly, he wanted her and that had been his reason for giving her the loan.

He had clearly changed since college. He was no longer the sensitive, charming man he'd been. He was hard and rough. He didn't care about her the way she thought he had back then—maybe it had just been a crush—but now all he wanted was her body. And she had agreed to give it to him.

She would not back out now for anything.

"Liv," he said evenly, "I'm only taking your feelings into consideration. The fact that you haven't had sex since then means . . ."

She glared at him.

"I don't want you to"—he clenched his jaw—"be with me if you don't want to."

"I *do* want to," she said fiercely, needing to convince him.

She grabbed his hand and pulled it to her thighs. He tried to pull away, but she pushed him between her legs, forcing his fingers against her folds.

"You can feel it, can't you?" She knew she was wet, and the feel of his fingers there sent a blind hunger through her that was almost too much to bear.

"Fuck, you are so wet."

He tried to draw his hand away again, but she grabbed his wrist and pulled it back.

"Then do something about it," she demanded through clenched teeth.

He stared at her, his eyes blazing with what looked like anger, but then he ripped his hand from her grip and pulled her into his arms. He cupped her head and drew her face to his. As soon as his lips brushed hers, his tongue invaded her mouth, driving inside her just as she was sure he wanted to drive his hard cock into her.

She melted against him. His erection, still confined within his jeans, pushed against her naked stomach, and she ached for him, at the same time as trepidation skittered through her. He cupped her ass and lifted her up. She wrapped her legs around him, enjoying the feel of his denim-covered shaft cradled between her legs as he carried her to the bed. He set her down on the edge and knelt in front of her. Then he reached for her chest and she expected him to tear open her shirt and tug down her bra to expose her naked breasts, but instead he pressed her back until she lay flat on the bed, her legs still dangling over the edge.

"Let's get this straight right now," he said, his gaze locking with hers as she watched him. "From here on forward, I am in charge and you will do exactly as I say. But if I do anything that makes you uncomfortable, tell me. Do you understand?"

She drew in a deep breath and nodded.

"Good. Now open your legs."

She obeyed, but despite her best efforts to remain calm, her earlier anxiety returned. Her gaze locked on the bulge in his jeans—the very large bulge—and she couldn't help tensing.

He rested his hand on her thigh and squeezed gently. "It's okay. Do you trust me?"

Trust? Despite her earlier thoughts about how she hadn't trusted anyone since "the incident," she realized that she did trust Shock. She didn't know why. He was a big, rough, tattooed biker. He was nothing like the man she'd known in college.

But she knew she could trust him.

She nodded.

"Now, do you want me to touch you?"

Her breath caught. Oh, God, she did. So much.

She nodded.

His fingers touched her intimate folds and she stifled a moan.

"Do you like me touching you?" he asked.

"Yes," she sighed.

He stroked along her sensitive flesh, then she watched as he leaned forward. His lips touched her slick folds and she moaned at the delightful sensation.

His tongue brushed against her and she jumped. He lifted his head and gazed at her. "Are you all right?"

"Yes. Please do it again."

He lowered his head and again his tongue glided over her. She arched to meet his mouth.

He tucked his arms under her knees and lifted, spreading her thighs wider. He pressed deeper into her, his breath brushing her skin. His tongue glided the length of her opening, then he drew her folds apart with his thumbs, exposing her clit.

He ran the tip of his tongue against it and fluttered. Wild sensations shot through her, sending her heart racing. His finger slipped inside her as he lapped at her clit. She tightened around him. He slid another finger inside and began to suck on her nub. She pushed the hair from her face as heat shimmered through her. She slid her hand over his head, weaving her fingers through his dark, wavy hair, then clinging to him as pleasure rocked through her.

"Oh, God."

His fingers continued to move inside her as heat blazed through her in waves. His tongue teased her, then he sucked again and she gasped. Blissful sensations swept over her and she groaned, her insides seeming to expand in a cataclysmic explosion of joy.

"Oh . . . Shock . . ." Then she wailed, tears welling from her eyes as the most intense pleasure she'd ever experienced blasted through her, tearing her from her body and casting her into a state of pure ecstasy.

She didn't know how long it took for her to settle back to the here-and-now, but the next thing she knew, Shock had pulled her into the bed and was lying beside her. He had shed his jeans and shirt, but the light cotton of his boxers remained a barrier between them. She still wore her shirt.

She rested her hand against his chest, then glided it down to his boxers, but he caught her wrist, then turned her away from him. Before she could feel rejected, he pulled her tightly to him, spooning against her back.

His cock, still big and hard, pressed into her behind.

"Now it's your turn," she murmured, trying to turn around, but he held her fast.

"Now it's time to go to sleep."

"But you're—"

"I said sleep. And as you agreed, while you're here, whatever I say in the bedroom goes. Are we clear?"

"Yes. Whatever you say," she murmured.

Shock didn't know how he could possibly fall asleep with her round, luscious ass pressed tight against his aching cock, the taste of her sweetness still on his lips.

He wanted her so bad, but he wouldn't take her now. Not after what she'd told him.

His stomach clenched at the idea of someone taking her against her will. She always had been headstrong, and often put herself into risky situations, but no matter what she had done or where she had been, that didn't give anyone the right to hurt her like that. To force her to do something she didn't want to do.

Guilt washed through him. Who the hell was he to talk? He had forced her into this situation. And now she was insisting on seeing it through. He'd given her the option to leave, but she felt the need to prove herself. It was a matter of pride with her.

Damn, if he could get out of this deal with her, he'd do it in a heartbeat. He'd still loan her the money, of course, but—

Fuck, who was he kidding? He wanted her, and he had for a long time. He wouldn't let her go now. Not until he'd had his fill of her. And she wanted him, too. She'd proven that tonight. They might both have issues, but the attraction between them—shit, the sheer primal need for each other—was undeniable.

She murmured softly in her sleep and he drew her closer to his body. His cock throbbed with the need to be inside her, but he ignored it as best he could.

This would be good for both of them. It would be a win-win situation. He would help her get over her sexual issues, and they would enjoy each other until the time was up.

Now all he had to do was find a way to fall asleep at night while being so close to her until they got to the point where he could drive his cock into her and relieve this intense yearning.

Liv woke up to an empty bed. She expected Shock's big, warm body close to her, but he was gone. She rolled onto her back and gazed at his empty pillow, then ran her hand across the impression where his head had been.

Last night had been . . . unexpected. He'd been so gentle and patient with her. So concerned.

And he'd totally rocked her world. Even though he hadn't actually had sex with her. She felt guilty that he had been left frustrated. He hadn't allowed her to do anything about it, but that only made her feel worse.

She pushed back the covers and walked to where her underwear still lay on the floor and pulled them on, then opened the door and peered out. She couldn't hear anyone in the house, so she walked down the hall, peering into rooms until she found the bathroom. She stripped off her shirt, bra, and panties and stepped into the shower, letting the warm water flow over her body. She washed and scrubbed every part of her. As her hands ran over her breasts, she thought of Shock's hands cupping them and caressing her. She soaped between her legs, remembering him touching her there. Licking and sucking. Giving her exquisite pleasure.

She leaned back against the tiled wall, thinking about Shock walking into the bathroom and stepping into the shower with her right now. Imagining him naked, his big cock, which she still hadn't seen, hanging heavy between his legs, then enlarging as he saw her naked body.

She closed her eyes and imagined him kissing her, his hard body pressing her against the tile wall, then the head of his cock nudging between her legs and pushing slowly inside.

There was a knock on the bathroom door and her eyes popped open.

"Who is it?" she asked.

The door opened just a little. "It's just you and me in the house, Liv," Shock said. "What are you doing in here?"

"Taking a shower." She knew he could hear the water.

He stayed on the other side of the door. "I can tell that. I just didn't know why you came to this one, since there's a private bathroom off our bedroom.

Our bedroom.

"I didn't know that."

"There are no towels in there. I'll go get you some." The door closed behind him.

A moment later he rapped on the door again and opened it a crack. "I'm bringing in the towels, but don't worry. I won't be able to see you through the frosted glass of the shower. Okay?"

"Yes," she answered.

He wouldn't see her. Well, he would, but just as a shadowy form. Would he be able to see the contours of her body? The shape of her breasts?

Would he be able to see that her nipples were hard from thinking of him touching her?

Would he know how wet she was . . . and not from the shower?

He opened the bathroom door and stepped inside.

Not if she didn't let him know.

She saw his form through the glass as he walked over to the long marble vanity and set down a stack of towels. Before her common sense could stop her, she stepped out from under the water and pulled open the glass door of the shower stall.

Shock heard the door of the shower open and his gaze jerked to her naked form.

Fuck, she was perfect. Her pert breasts were full and round, droplets of water glistening on her satiny skin. He watched one drop glide down the swell of flesh and for one second seem suspended from her nipple before falling, landing on her stomach, then continuing down to her fully shaved pussy.

He felt a little guilty making that one of the requirements in the contract, but he hadn't known about her inexperience. He did it to push her a little, hoping the demands would turn her on.

His cock swelled and he knew that if she didn't cover up soon, he'd do something he shouldn't. Like pushing her into something she wasn't ready for yet.

He grabbed one of the big, fluffy bath towels he'd brought in and shook it open, then held it out to her like a curtain.

She shook her head. "I'm not finished showering yet."

But she stepped out of the stall and pushed the towel aside, then stepped toward him, her gaze locked with his. She stroked his cheek, then stepped in closer and drew his head toward her. The moment their lips brushed, he knew he was in trouble.

She closed the small distance between them, pressed her wet body against his, and wrapped her arms around him, her tongue gliding between his lips. His arms slid around her of their own volition. The feel of her naked skin was his undoing.

He deepened the kiss and pulled her closer still, her soft breasts crushed against him, her puckered nipples driving him wild. His hand found a breast, cupping it in his palm. She arched against him.

Oh, God, he'd died and gone to heaven.

His cock grew painfully hard pushing against his jeans like an animal intent on escape. And if it did get free, he knew exactly where it would seek refuge.

Gaining his senses, he summoned every ounce of will he could find and drew away from her.

"Liv, no."

She stroked his shoulders, then moved her hands down his chest.

"Why?" The heat in her sky-blue eyes burned through him.

"You know why. You're not ready for this."

"I'd say speak for yourself . . ."

He jerked as one hand suddenly moved to his cock.

". . . but it's clear that you're ready, too."

He captured the hand on his throbbing cock, and the one still on his chest and held them away from him.

"I'm not doing this," he insisted.

She didn't try to pull her hands away, just sank to her knees in front of him, gliding her cheek over the aching bulge in his pants, then resting her face against it. Shit, this was worse than her hand stroking him. Then she turned her head and nuzzled the denim. He almost died when she kissed the fabric, the only thing standing between her lips and his twitching cock.

He pulled her to her feet, glaring at her, but she leaned forward, her naked body hot against him.

"Liv . . ." he said in exasperation.

"Shock, you started something last night we didn't finish."

"And we're not finishing it. Not now."

She arched an eyebrow. "When?"

"I don't know," he said. "When you're ready."

"And wouldn't I know when I'm ready better than you?"

At the flare of rebellion in her eyes, he answered, "Then when *I'm* ready. You promised to obey me, remember? That was part of the deal."

She sighed. "Yes, it was. Please let go of my hands. Or do you want to keep restraining me?"

He released her hands, hoping she'd move her hot, sexy body away from him. And she did take a step back. Making it worse. At the sight of her naked glory, his cock stiffened even more.

"You remember what you made me leave on the list?"

"What?" he asked, uncomprehending, his brain foggy from the haze of desire.

"In the sex contract. You remember what I was going to cross off and you didn't let me?"

He stared at her blankly.

"The word that started with an *f.*"

Did she mean "fuck"? Then he remembered her pen resting on the word "fellatio," ready to cross it out.

"Uh, yeah."

Her hand found his iron-hard cock again, which had swelled to the point of pain at the thought of her lips around him.

"I want to do that now."

"But . . ."

She sank to her knees, caressing his shaft. "Come on, you clearly want me to do it." Then she gazed up at him, her big, blue eyes showing vulnerability. "Shock, you made me feel something very special last night. Please let me do that in return."

Her fingers grasped the tab of his zipper and drew it down slowly.

Everything in him told him to stop her. She was innocent. Inexperienced. She should not be doing this because of a contract.

But he couldn't move. The sight of her naked and on her knees in front of him, gazing at his open jeans as if there were a treasure inside, turned him on too fucking much.

Then her fingers slid inside and wrapped around him and he groaned softly.

She drew him out and just stared at his cock.

Liv had never experienced anything like it. His cock was thick and solid in her hand, but the skin was soft as silk. She wrapped her fingers around it and stroked its length, feeling the soft skin glide over a burning-hot steel shaft.

She gazed at his eyes, which had turned to simmering dark chocolate as he watched her.

She wasn't quite sure what to do, so she continued to stroke him. His eyelids closed, then opened again. She slipped the fingers of her other hand under his balls and cupped them.

"Oh, baby, that feels nice," he murmured.

Encouraged, she fondled his balls gently as she stroked his cock.

"Do you like this?" she asked.

"Fuck, yeah."

"What would you like me to do now? I want to make you feel good."

"Ohhh. Lick my cock, baby. Just under the head. I love that."

She pressed her tongue to the tip of him, then glided down the head to the lower ridge of the mushroom shape, thrilled at the sound of his soft moan, then she ran her tongue under the ridge. Around one side, then the other. She did that a couple of times, then squeezed his shaft and glided her lips over the head, as big as a clementine, and took it in her mouth. He groaned.

His hand slid over her head, then forked through her hair. She ran her tongue around the underside of the ridge while he was in her mouth.

"Baby, that feels so good."

She stroked his shaft while her tongue teased the head of his cock, still in the warm confines of her mouth. She felt his hand guiding her toward his body, so she took him deeper. He was big for her mouth, but she glided down his shaft about halfway, then slowly glided back. Then she glided deep again. She started to move her hand, which still clutched his shaft, following her mouth.

She caressed his balls gently as she glided up and down his cock to his increasing moans. She moved faster, gazing up at him. His eyelids had fallen closed again, and his head was tipped back.

Now her mouth slipped off the end of his cock but she continued stroking him with her hand.

"Are you getting close?" she asked.

"Fuck, yeah, baby. Keep going. I'll let you know."

"Shock, that other item I crossed off? The very next one."

His eyes opened and his gaze locked on her. "Yeah?"

"Ignore that."

"Oh, fuck."

He grasped his cock and pushed it to her lips, sliding it inside. She sucked on the bulbous tip for mere seconds before he groaned and jerked forward, then hot liquid erupted from his cockhead, filling her mouth. Startled, she had to stop herself from pulling away, but the feel of him coming to climax in her mouth sent need ricocheting through her. She swallowed the salty-sweet liquid, then again as he continued to fill her. She sucked on him until he had nothing else to give her. Then she ran her tongue around the head and drew away.

He tugged her to her feet and drove his tongue between her lips, probing her mouth with ardor.

When he finally released her, she gazed into his melting-chocolate eyes, as he stared at her with adoration.

"I . . . made you happy . . ." It had begun as a question, but from the look on his face, there was no doubt in her mind.

"Yes, you did." Then he glided his tongue into her mouth again and kissed her so passionately, she thought she'd melt into a little puddle on the floor.

Finally, he drew away.

"Once you finish your shower, come downstairs. I'll have breakfast ready."

When Liv descended the stairs, she could smell the aroma of fresh biscuits. And bacon.

She walked into the bright, spacious kitchen and was

greeted by the sight of Shock pulling a tray of hot biscuits from the oven.

"Grab a cup of coffee and sit at the table." Shock tipped the tray so the biscuits slid into a napkin-lined basket, then he covered them with another napkin to keep them warm.

She poured a cup from the pot in the coffeemaker and sat down at the table. Shock joined her a moment later with the basket of biscuits and two plates with omelets and bacon.

She tried a bite. "This is delicious."

"Thanks."

And that was the extent of their conversation during breakfast. She wanted to talk. To find out more about him and how he had dealt with the falling-out with his family, but she wasn't sure how to start without hitting a nerve. And talking about their current situation was touchy, too. He seemed more affected by her innocence than she'd thought he'd be, but it shouldn't have surprised her. She knew at the heart of his lectures was a protectiveness toward her. Knowing she'd been . . . taken advantage of would bring that out in him in spades.

So they ate in silence. When they were both finished, she helped him clear away the dishes, then she loaded the dishwasher as he washed the pans. She closed the dishwasher and watched him wipe his hands on the towel.

"So, what are we going to do today?" she asked.

At his hesitation, she moved closer and ran her hands up his chest. "Maybe we should go back to the bedroom."

"Yes, that's exactly what we should do."

His words were encouraging, but not his tone. She stroked down his chest to his stomach, but he grasped her hand before she could glide over his growing cock.

"Because you're going to pack."

Her heart sank. "Why?" But she knew why.

"Because this ends now. I'm taking you home."

Part Two

"No." Liv stared at him defiantly.

Shock glared at her. "What do you mean 'No'?"

She crossed her arms over her chest. "I mean I'm not going."

"The hell you aren't." He grabbed her wrist and yanked her with him, then dragged her up the stairs. He pushed her into the bedroom. "Now pack."

Instead, she went and sat on the bed.

"Liv, I'm not kidding."

She stared at him speculatively.

"Let's just talk about this for a minute," she said in her most reasonable tone.

"We don't need to talk. I've made my decision."

"Well, that's the whole problem, isn't it? You've made *your* decision."

"You said you'd do whatever I say."

"In the bedroom," she clarified. "And we both know that meant during sex, but now you don't want to have sex with me."

"That's not true."

She pursed her lips. "It is true, at least since you found out I'm not experienced."

"It's not your lack of experience that's the issue."

"What then?" Anger bubbled inside her. "Because of what happened to me?"

Her heart ached. He was judging her. Because she'd gotten herself into a stupid situation. And that stupid guy had taken advantage of that situation and . . . Damn it, because of that, she had stayed away from relationships. Had been afraid to let anyone close.

God damn it, she was so broken.

"Liv, why don't you understand? I don't want to be the second man who forces you into sex."

"What?" She stared at him in shock.

"I coerced you to sign a contract. To have sex with me. You needed money and I took advantage of the situation." He picked up her backpack and set it on the bed. "That was wrong. And even worse now that I know what happened to you." He stared at her. "I'm no better than that guy."

"Shock, it's not the same thing. I know you would never . . ."

She frowned and shook her head. She wanted to take his hand and tell him how much she'd wanted to be with him all those years ago. How much she'd dreamed of him taking her into his arms and kissing her. Touching her.

But after the incident happened . . . she'd been afraid. Afraid to be touched. Afraid to trust.

So she'd pushed him away. Subtly at first. She found

excuses to slow down the activities they did together. Like running in the park, which they used to do a few times a week, became twice a week, then once. And she'd stopped going with him to see the old movies they showed at the campus center on Tuesdays. They weren't dates, just two friends spending time together, but she'd always wanted them to be more. Before "the incident."

Then, when he'd seemed to feel her slipping away, he'd actually asked her out on a real date. And she'd flatly refused, telling him she just wanted to stay friends. Over the following month, she'd discontinued all their time together, even studying, until they saw each other only in class.

She hadn't been able to handle more than that. Not while she longed to be closer to him. If they could have truly just been friends . . .

But she'd wanted more . . . and couldn't handle that.

She realized he'd unzipped her bag and had grabbed a handful of clothes that she'd unpacked into an empty drawer in the dresser before she'd gone down to breakfast and was pushing them into the empty backpack.

"Shock?"

At her hesitant tone, he glanced her way.

"Please stop," she implored. "I don't want to go home." She reached for his callused hand and held it in her own. "What we've started here . . . it's been good for me. I'm . . ."—she dropped her gaze, letting it fall to their joined hands—"broken."

He pushed the backpack aside and sat down beside her, tightening his hand around hers. "No, Liv, that's not true."

She gazed at his warm, brown eyes. "It is true. When he did that to me, he broke something inside me." She dropped her gaze to their hands once more, drawing comfort from the gentle pressure of his fingers. "I didn't *choose* not to have sex all these years. I was *afraid* to have sex." She looked up again, meeting his somber gaze. "But I'm not afraid with you. What we did yesterday . . . and this morning was exciting." She squeezed his hand. "I'm not trying to put a huge weight on your shoulders or anything, but I really think that you can help me." She raised their joined hands and stroked his against her cheek. "Please, let me stay and finish what we started."

"Fuck, Liv . . ."

Suddenly, she was pulled into his arms, his mouth covering hers. She melted against him, her mouth opening to him.

Need washed through her and all she could think about was being naked in his arms, then opening to him as his big, heavy cock glided inside her. Filling her. Bringing her to heights even greater, and more fulfilling, than last night. If that was even possible.

He broke the kiss to ask, "Liv, are you sure?"

She took his hand and slid it over her breast, then pressed his fingers closed around it.

"So sure."

He moaned and deepened the kiss.

Her heart beat wildly as he pulled her farther onto the bed, then leaned in and claimed her lips again, pressing her onto her back. She could hear his heart pounding in his chest, too. And a roaring in her ears.

She pressed his hand against her breast again, but the roar grew louder, then became thunderous.

"Oh, fuck." Shock slipped away from her and peered out the window.

"What is it?" she asked, just wanting him to come back.

"It's Steele and the others. They just arrived."

As Liv followed Shock downstairs, she tossed her hair over her shoulder nervously. Her cheeks were flushed and she was sure that the newcomers would know exactly what she and Shock had been doing.

Of course they'd know. That was why Shock had brought her here a day early, to give them some time alone together. Shock hadn't said as much, but it wasn't hard to figure out.

What had he told them about her? Did they know Shock had loaned her money? Did they know she was here to fulfill a contract?

The front door opened and she heard loud male voices and the sound of heavy biker boots on the ceramic tile floor of the entrance.

"Hey, Steele. Good ride up?" Shock asked as he stepped off the stairway and into the large foyer with Liv right behind him. Five large tattooed men in jeans and two women, dressed similarly to Liv, stood in the entrance.

A tall man with dark wavy hair and exceptional good looks who Liv hadn't met yet nodded. "Always." His blue eyes locked on Liv, sending her heart stuttering. This was the leader of Shock's group of biker friends. "This is Olivia, I take it."

"Everyone calls me Liv."

She held out her hand and Steele shook it. The feel of his big, powerful hand around hers flustered her. When he released it, she drew it back and sent a quick glance to Shock for reassurance.

"Liv, you already met Wild Card, Magic, and Dom."

She nodded to them and Wild Card smiled. The other two nodded.

"And this is Rip," Shock said, gesturing to the fifth man.

Rip's hair was dark and wavy and his eyes a deep midnight blue. Dense, coarse whiskers shadowed his face, except where a two-inch scar slashed across his cheek, but his warm smile softened his dangerous good looks.

He took her hand and shook it. "Nice to meet you, Liv."

"And this is Raven and Tempest," Shock said as the two women stepped toward her.

Both women had long dark hair, but Raven's was as black as a raven's wing, which was undoubtedly how she'd gotten her nickname. Tempest was a little taller, with heart-shaped lips. Both were stunning.

"I love your jeans," Raven said. "I'd love to get a pair like that."

Rip slid his arm around her waist and drew her tight to his side. "And I would love you to wear a pair like that." He nuzzled her neck and she laughed.

Tempest held out her hand. "Nice to meet you."

Liv shook her hand and relaxed a little. She didn't know how to read the men's attitudes, but the women made her feel that she'd been accepted.

"Nice place." Dom glanced around the foyer, which opened onto a large living room with dark honey-colored hardwood floors. "Bedrooms upstairs?"

"Yeah, there are five." Shock stepped aside as the new-comers headed upstairs with their bags.

As the others were walking up the stairs, Shock took her hand and led her down the hall. "They'll probably be hungry, so I'll make some sandwiches. You can sit out on the deck if you'd like. Or go for a swim."

"No, I'll help."

In the kitchen, he pulled out a couple loaves of bread and cold cuts and veggies from the fridge, and they began putting together a plate of sandwiches.

"There aren't enough bedrooms for everyone. Will some of them be sleeping on the couch?"

"There are enough. Raven's with Rip, and Tempest's with Steele."

"That leaves one short."

He placed some slices of ham on the bread she'd buttered. "Dom and Magic will bunk in together."

"Oh." She cut a tomato into thin slices and arranged them on some of the sandwiches.

Fifteen minutes later, the others started trailing down the stairs. Shock placed the sandwiches on the table with plates and then grabbed beers for everyone.

"The backyard looks pretty nice," Magic said. "I saw a pool out there."

"And a hot tub," Tempest said with a smile. "I'm going for a swim after lunch."

"There's a lake just down the way, too," Shock said.

"My kind of place." Steele smiled.

As they finished their sandwiches, they cleared their dishes and Shock put them in the dishwasher.

"Since you have this all handled," Raven said, "I'm going for a swim."

"Me, too." Tempest followed her to the stairs.

"Why don't you go put your swimsuit on?" Shock suggested. "I'm basically done here."

"Okay." Liv glanced up at him. "Are you going, too?"

The thought of getting into the skimpy bikini Shock had had the personal shopper buy for her and wearing it in front of all these hulking men made her a little nervous. She knew she'd be safe with Shock, but she still wasn't comfortable with being on display.

He glanced at her and seemed to read her nervousness. "Yeah, sure. I'll come up now."

Magic and Wild Card, who were still sitting at the table finishing their beers, grinned and glanced at each other as Shock took her hand. They were obviously assuming . . . but she shouldn't care. They could assume whatever they wanted. She would do her best not to let it throw her.

She trotted up the stairs with Shock behind her. Once in the room with the door closed behind her, she walked to the dresser and pulled out the black and white bikini. She tossed it on the bed and pulled off her T-shirt without even thinking. She reached behind her back to unfasten

her bra, then remembered that Shock was standing only
a few feet away.

She glanced around. He was staring at her, mesmerized.

Sure, he'd seen her totally naked, but that didn't mean
she was comfortable just casually changing in front of him.
She grabbed the bathing suit and headed to the en suite
bathroom, then closed the door behind her. Once she had
changed, she grabbed a brush from the vanity counter
and brushed her long hair. She opened a small drawer and
found some covered elastics, so she pulled her hair into a
ponytail and braided it.

When she returned to the bedroom, Shock stood in
royal-blue swim trunks. He whistled, his hot gaze gliding
the length of her mostly naked body.

"Very nice."

"I take it you like your own taste in bathing suits."

He smiled and stepped toward her. His hands glided
down her naked sides and his lips brushed her shoulder.
"It's more that I like my taste in women." His arm hooked
around her waist and he drew her near. As he kissed her
skin lightly, shivers danced across her flesh.

"I think we should go downstairs."

Shock nuzzled the base of her neck, making her knees
go weak. "I'm sure they won't miss us for a few minutes."

His hand cupped her breast, lifting it slightly, then his
thumb found her tightening nipple. When he brushed over
it, she had to stop herself from gasping.

"Please, Shock. No." When she glanced up at him, he
frowned. "I know I said I'd obey you—"

He shook his head. "I just want to know. Have you changed your mind again?" His hand slid away. "I can take you home right now if you like."

"No, I don't want to go."

God, he must think she'd decided not to have sex with him after all.

"Nothing's changed except timing." She drew his hand back to her and tucked it under her breast. "I don't want our first time to be a few stolen moments."

"So you want your first real time to be special. Maybe candlelight and roses?"

She gazed into his warm brown eyes. "No." She stroked his whisker-roughened cheek. "I just want you, and enough privacy and time that we don't feel rushed."

She rose on her tiptoes and brushed her lips against his. He drew her tight to his body and deepened the kiss. She felt a growing bulge in his trunks pressing against her.

"I'm sure that can be arranged." He nuzzled her ear.

"Well, from the feel of things, you might not be going downstairs right away." She was his sexual partner, which meant she had responsibilities. She glided her hand down his stomach, then over his bulge. "Do you want me to do something about this?"

But he grabbed her hand and drew it away. "Look, baby. I understand if you want to wait, and yes, I'm hard being this close to you, especially in that fine little scrap of cloth you're wearing, but you don't have to suck me off because of it. Okay?"

She bit her lip. "But—"

"No buts. Let's go downstairs."

She glanced at his erection, clearly visible in his trunks. How could he just walk out there like that? But once they were in the hall, he opened a closet and pulled out a couple of large beach towels and handed one to her, then draped the other over his arm, covering his hard-on.

She smiled, then followed him down the stairs and into the kitchen. Tempest stood at the counter, tall and sexy in a hot-pink bikini.

"Hey, you two. Want to help me?" Tempest asked. "I made a pitcher of margaritas. I could use help carrying out the glasses."

The three of them walked outside onto the patio with the glasses and a frosty pitcher and set them on the big round teak table. Soon they were all relaxing by the pool, enjoying the afternoon sun.

The backyard was huge, with beautiful landscaping that was definitely well maintained. There were lots of plants and brightly colored flowers, different sitting areas, a large in-ground pool, and a lake with a small beach about a hundred yards from the deck. A hot tub was tucked in a corner, kept secluded from the lake by flowering bushes.

Shock took a sip of the margarita Tempest poured for him, then walked to the pool, dropped the towel, and dove into the water.

"So you've known Shock since college?" Tempest asked as she sat down across from Liv.

"Yes, we were study partners and friends."

"And now you're more," Raven said with a smile as she moved from one of the lounge chairs near the table to pour herself a drink.

Liv wondered how much they knew about her and Shock's current situation. Did they know that he had a contract for her to be his sexual slave? Her cheeks flushed. Or did they just think she and Shock had started seeing each other? But would she really start riding with them—for a whole month—if they'd only just reconnected, and after being just friends?

No matter what they knew, they must wonder at how fast things had moved between her and Shock.

She wanted to explain that things hadn't worked out in college, but that they'd always been attracted to each other and this was their opportunity. She felt the need to justify why she had jumped into bed with him. But there was no real way to explain it, so better to leave everything unsaid. Anyway, whatever she said probably wouldn't match what Shock would say. He might want to protect her feelings by not making it seem as if she'd just spread her legs because he loaned her money, and that all he really wanted was a brief physical relationship with her—a month, to be precise.

Who was she kidding? He had probably told his buddies everything.

"Liv, are you okay?" Tempest asked, concern in her blue eyes.

"Oh, yeah, sure."

"You seemed to zone out there for a moment."

"Sorry, it's just a bit overwhelming meeting all of you." She glanced toward the big tattooed bikers hanging around the side of the pool, talking. "And the men are, well, a bit intimidating."

"I know what you mean. I thought that at first, too." Tempest placed her hand on Liv's. "They may be big and rough-looking, but believe me, there's nothing to be worried about."

"Yeah, Liv." Raven smiled. "They only bite if invited."

"Rave, you're just going to scare her," Tempest admonished.

The two women really got along well together. Liv could see that, and wished that she could be a part of their circle. But she would be here for only a month, so it would be better if she kept her distance. No point making connections she would only lose in the end. That would just make it harder when she left.

She glanced toward the pool and noticed Magic walking toward them. His gaze dipped to her breasts. The attention made her feel desirable, but also left her nervous, as it always did when men eyed her.

He smiled at her and poured himself a drink from the frosty pitcher. She noticed the tattoo on his wrist as he lifted his glass. It was a band of thorns that were inked to look as though they pierced his skin, with blood dripping from the punctures. A thorny vine spiraled up his arm, leaving droplets of blood along the way, and words were written in script inside the vine. Her gaze followed it over his shoulder, then down his chest and . . . *oh, my* . . . she realized that the tattoo on his chest depicted the thorns pulling back his skin, exposing his heart beneath. Although it was just an artistic design on his skin, it looked disturbingly real.

Magic turned toward the pool at the sound of someone

diving in, and she read the words on his arm. *My secrets are my own.*

Wow, there had to be a lot of meaning there.

She glanced around at the other men and the tattoos on their naked chests and arms, but she couldn't make them out from here.

Shock had gotten out of the pool and walked toward her, then downed his margarita.

"Babe, I've got some stuff to do. Stay out here and socialize. I'll be back soon." Then he disappeared through the French doors into the house.

She stared after him, every part of her wanting to slip inside as well. The contract had only stated that she had to follow his commands in the bedroom, but he wanted her to stay here, so she would.

It turned out to be a pleasant afternoon. The others joked and chatted, and they made an effort to draw her into their small talk, and she made an effort to be sociable but was a little inept. After working long hours and taking care of her sister and grandma, she found that she had lost the knack for socializing.

Liv watched as the men casually touched or stroked Tempest and Raven. Mostly it was their own partners—Steele with Tempest and Rip with Raven—but sometimes the other men would pat an arm or brush against a long, feminine leg.

Not with Liv, though. They didn't approach her or do anything to intimidate her in any way. In fact, she almost felt as if Steele, whom she knew was the leader, was keeping a watchful eye over her.

Finally, Shock returned and sat down beside her. She

was relieved. As nice as everyone was, she was finding the effort to interact with them all tiring. Maybe now she could make her escape.

"Having a good time?" he asked.

She nodded. "But I've been out in the sun for quite a while, so I should probably go inside."

Shock sipped the beer he'd carried out with him. He was pleased that Liv was still outside. He had fully expected that telling her to stay outside would cause her to defiantly go into the house as soon as he left. Ordinarily, she'd defy him to his face, but with all these people she didn't know, she would have waited. But instead she'd stayed outside and when he'd glanced out periodically while he'd been on the phone, he'd gotten the impression that she'd made a real effort to be sociable.

"That's probably a good idea." He smiled. "I wouldn't want you to get a sunburn."

Her gaze locked on his, then jerked away. He was sure she was thinking, just as he was, about what would happen tonight between them. He was disappointed that she seemed to be back to her skittish self, though. Had her desire to be with him been a short-lived thing, only based on the brief sexual excitement that had blossomed between them this morning?

Hopefully, what he had planned tonight would re-ignite their passion.

She stood up and said good-bye to the others, then walked to the house. He followed quickly, before his arousal at the thought of tonight became too physically obvious.

"You don't have to come in with me," she said at the door.

"I want to."

She glanced up at him as if she expected he would follow her to the room, then ravage her as soon as the door closed. Which was exactly what he would like to do. But wouldn't.

He followed her up the stairs, his cock swelling more at the sight of her sexy, swaying ass. Once he followed her into the room and closed the door, he couldn't help but pull her into his arms and kiss her. She didn't push him away, and her breathing accelerated, but she was stiff in his arms.

He glided his tongue into her as he pulled her tighter to him, and she relaxed into his embrace, melting against him.

She gazed at him with wide blue eyes. He could tell she expected that it was going to happen right now. That he was about to take her in her first real sexual encounter with a man. One in which she had a say, that is. Not that she seemed to think she did.

He grasped her shoulders. "Liv, we're not doing anything now. This evening I'm going to take you out for a nice dinner, and—"

"You don't have to buy me dinner. I'm a sure thing, remember?"

He laughed, then gave her a peck on the cheek. "Okay, well, let's just say that I want to make sure you have a good dinner so you can keep up your strength."

* * *

Liv watched as Shock lay down on the bed and started to read a book.

Finally, she grabbed her tablet from her purse and sat in the chair by the window, pulled up a book of her own, and started to read. After about an hour, the doorbell rang. Shock got up from the bed and headed to the door, but as soon as he opened it, Wild Card, still in his bathing suit, appeared with a large, flat box in his hand.

"This just came for you," he said, handing the box to Shock.

"Thanks."

Shock closed the door and put the box on the bed. He pulled a pocketknife from his pocket and cut the string tied around the box, then lifted off the lid.

"These things are for you to wear tonight. Why don't you go in the bathroom and get ready? I'll meet you downstairs when you're done."

She walked to the bed and lifted a silky black dress from the box. "I take it we're going out for a fancy dinner."

He smiled. "I told you, I just want to make sure you're well fed to keep up your strength."

She picked up the box and carried it into the en suite bathroom, which had a dressing area with a bench and mirrors. She set the box on the marble counter in front of the mirrors and pulled out the items. There was the dress, which was long and slinky, and very low-cut. Then there were some black, lacy items with narrow red ribbon trim. She lifted the bra, which was strapless, and the cups were only half the normal size. The panties were tiny, the back just a narrow string topped with a triangle of lace. Her cheeks flushed at the thought of how much of her would be left exposed in that underwear.

There was also a matching garter belt and black stockings. Then she found a pair of multicolored sequined shoes with stiletto heels and red soles.

She put on some makeup and brushed her shoulder-length honey-blonde hair, wondering if she should put it up, but all she had with her were elastics, and a ponytail wasn't really the look she'd choose for an elegant evening.

She stripped down and put on the underwear. Oh, God, the bra didn't even cover her nipples. Unwilling to look at herself in the mirror yet, she sat down and drew on the silky stockings. She'd never worn a garter belt before, so she struggled a bit getting the stockings attached, but finally stood up and glanced at her reflection.

Her cheeks flushed at the sight of the ultra-sexy woman in the mirror.

That could not be her.

She stepped into the shoes and her body transformed again, her ass and breasts appearing more pronounced. And even sexier.

Good heavens, Shock was going to see her like this.

She turned and grabbed the dress, needing to cover herself. She slipped it over her head and felt the silky fabric glide over her body and fall into place, then turned to the mirror again.

She could hardly believe it. She had covered her nakedness, but not changed the level of sexiness one whit. The long, slinky dress hugged every curve, making her feel essentially naked.

How could she walk out of this room and down the stairs in front of everyone? And then into a restaurant full of people?

But she had to. This was what Shock wanted her to do, so she would do it.

She opened the door of the bathroom, wondering if Shock was still in the bedroom, but he wasn't. He'd said to meet him downstairs, so she drew back her shoulders and stepped out of the room, then walked down the stairs with her head held high.

She heard a whistle as she approached the bottom of the staircase and glanced around. Steele stood in the foyer watching her. But there was no sign of Shock.

"You look stunning," he said.

"Thank you." Despite her best efforts, her shoulders sagged.

A moment later, there was a knock at the door. Steele opened it, then turned to her.

"It's for you, Liv."

"Me?"

She walked to the door, and her breath caught as she saw Shock standing there, excruciatingly handsome in an expensive-looking suit, his hair combed neatly into place.

"Good evening, Liv." He held out his elbow. "I'm here to pick you up for our date."

Dazed, she put her hand on his elbow, wondering how she would get onto the bike in this dress without hiking it up to her thighs.

But sitting in the driveway was a shiny black limousine.

She was going to protest at the lavish treatment, but she realized that was ridiculous. For the two of them to ride the motorcycle in these clothes would be crazy.

The chauffeur opened the door for them and Shock took her hand and helped her into the car, then slid in beside her. The supple leather seats were large and comfortable. As soon as the car started moving, Shock opened a compartment, revealing a bottle of champagne on ice inside, and popped the cork, then poured the bubbly liquid into two flutes. He handed her one and she sipped it.

Typically, she'd never cared for champagne—she'd drink it to be sociable when celebrating something—but this was not like any she'd ever had before. It was like ambrosia.

Suddenly, she realized she'd finished the glass and Shock was filling it again.

"You know, I already told you. You don't need to get me drunk." She sipped the wine again and giggled as the bubbles tickled her nose. "I'm a sure thing."

"I'm not intending to get you drunk, and if you think that's going to happen, I'll take it from you right now."

But when he playfully reached for her glass, Liv held it away.

"No, no. I like it."

He leaned in close to nuzzle her ear. "I haven't told you yet how incredibly sexy you look in that dress."

She took another sip of champagne and giggled again. "Yeah? You should see me out of it."

He smiled. "I am looking forward to that."

She tried to take another sip, but the glass was empty

again. She grabbed the bottle and filled it herself, then leaned close to him. "Did you know that the bra is only half there?" She giggled. "My nipples are totally exposed."

She glanced down at herself and realized her nipples were hard and poking out, the outlines clearly visible through the fabric.

"Oh, my."

She took another sip from her flute.

"Here, Liv, why don't you give me that?" Shock slipped the glass from her fingers and put it back in the wet bar.

"And the panties are less than useless in covering anything. I might as well be naked under this dress."

"Liv, you're painting a mental image I'm having trouble ignoring."

She glanced at his pants and saw the huge bulge straining against the fine wool fabric.

"Oh, it's so hard. Does it hurt when that happens?" She rested her hand on his erection and stroked it.

He grabbed her hand and held it, stopping her from touching him. "Only when you do that."

She was confused. "I'm hurting you?"

"No, baby, I just mean you make it get bigger, and that makes it hurt when it's confined."

"We just need to let it out," she said as she sank to the floor and unzipped his fly, then pushed her hand inside. The feel of his hot, hard flesh in her fingers sent heat searing through her. But as she leaned down to take him in her mouth, he lifted her back onto the seat.

"Liv, just slow down, sweetie. We've got all night. I don't want to rush anything."

He disengaged her hand and tucked himself away, zipping up his fly again.

"Oh, that's so sweet." She leaned close and nuzzled the base of his neck.

His arm came around her and he drew her close to his side. "We're almost at the restaurant."

A few minutes later, the car stopped in front of an elegant hotel and the driver opened the door. Shock got out and helped Liv out of the car, then led her to the entrance. They took a glass elevator up the tall building, then were led by the maître d' to a table with a stunning view of several small lakes surrounded by trees below. On the other side of the restaurant, the view was of the skyline of the small city. She wasn't sure of the name of it, but remembered driving through it on the way to Shock's country house.

Shock pulled out the chair for her and once she'd sat down in the comfy seat, he pushed it in for her. The restaurant was elegant, with white linen tablecloths and tall, tapered candles on each table. The waiter poured them glasses of ice water as Shock sat down across from her.

"It's a very nice restaurant," she said.

Her head was spinning a little, but the waiter brought bread and Shock cut a bun from the basket and buttered it, then set it on her side plate.

Shock ordered for both of them—she didn't really pay attention to what, but when the waiter set a bowl of lobster bisque in front of her, she glanced at Shock.

"I love lobster bisque." She'd only had it once, since it wasn't the kind of thing she could usually afford, but she had never forgotten it.

He smiled. "I know."

She didn't ask him how he knew. Maybe she had told him when they'd known each other in college, but she couldn't believe he'd remember.

"Shock, you were my friend in college, but I know you wanted to be more. I'm really sorry about that."

He raised an eyebrow at her bluntness and she realized the champagne was still affecting her.

"I'm sorry. I shouldn't have brought that up."

He put down his soup spoon. "No. Since you have brought it up, I'm sorry, too." He leaned forward. "Liv, I never understood it. I was so attracted to you, and I was sure you were attracted to me, too."

She stared down at her soup and took another spoonful. Then she nodded. "I was . . ." She glanced up at him. "I am."

"Then why?" His gaze bored through her. "Why did you turn me down when I asked you out? And why did you drift away from me right after? If I hadn't insisted, you would have let our friendship die completely."

She frowned. "I'm sorry. I really am. But . . ." She sucked in a deep breath, not sure she could continue this. Especially not here in this public place.

"But what, Liv? That really did a number on me. I want to know."

Shock watched her. He hadn't intended to push her on this tonight, but she'd brought it up. He knew he was taking advantage a little, but with the champagne making her more open, maybe he'd finally get the answer he'd needed for so many years.

"It was just . . ." She hesitated, then took a sip of water.

She gazed at him and the pain in her eyes disturbed him. "It was around the time . . ."

Fuck, tears were welling in her eyes.

God damn it.

"Liv, did the thing that happened to you . . ." He clenched his fists. "Is that when it happened?"

She nodded, wiping a tear from her eyes.

He felt totally helpless. He wanted to protect her, but there was nothing he could do about something that had happened to her in the past.

Except help her move forward.

"God, Liv, I'm sorry. I didn't mean to get you upset."

She shook her head, wiping another tear away.

He handed her his napkin. "Here, use this."

She looked at it hesitantly. "I don't want to ruin it."

"It's just a piece of cloth. It'll wash."

She dabbed at her eyes, clearly trying not to leave streaks of black mascara on the pristine white linen.

"Do you want to leave?" he asked.

"No," she said quickly. "This is so lovely. I don't want to ruin it. It's so nice that . . ." She smiled tremulously. "That you wanted to make tonight special."

He took her hand and cradled it between his own. It felt so soft and delicate, so fragile.

"Of course." He kissed the back of her hand.

The waiter approached and poured them more water. She withdrew her hand and continued eating her soup.

They hardly talked for the rest of dinner, simply enjoyed the fine cuisine and the wine, which Shock ordered by the glass so it didn't get ahead of her.

Finally, they finished their meal and enjoyed the live background music over coffee.

"Shall we go?" Shock asked.

Liv nodded and stood up, then rested her hand on the arm he offered and walked with him to the elevator. Every man in the room watched the sexy swaying of her body as they strolled through the room.

The dress really did look spectacular on her, and he'd been trying to ignore the outlines of her nipples through the cloth ever since she'd made him so pointedly aware of them in the limo. He'd had trouble succeeding, his cock rising and falling like a tide. When the conversation had turned serious, he'd forgotten for a while, focused on her pain, but sitting across from her, it didn't take long into dinner for his gaze to wander to those little buds again.

Now, as she walked toward the elevator, his cock started to swell, and when he pushed the elevator button and she turned away from him as one of the elevators in another column dinged, he hardened to full readiness at the sight of her round ass, with no panty line, there in front of him. The slinky fabric clung to her fine form, and reminded him if he stroked over that fabric, there would be practically nothing between him and her naked skin.

Liv stepped into the elevator and he followed. She reached to push the button for the lobby, but he pressed the one for the nineteenth floor instead. She glanced at him in surprise.

"You didn't think I'd take you back to the house with all those people there, did you?" He pulled a key card from his pocket. "I had us checked in earlier and the chauffeur gave me this when he picked us up."

Liv drew in a deep breath. She had thought they were going back to the house, and had expected to have the drive home to calm herself, but now she had only moments until she found herself alone in a bedroom with Shock.

No matter how much she wanted to be with him, she still felt supremely nervous about this. It was not just the anxiety that her long-instilled fear would get the best of her—and if it didn't, that the act would hurt—but . . . what if she didn't please him? Or that she didn't meet his expectations, which was actually pretty likely. After all, he'd wanted her for years. He must have built up an idea of what it would be like to be with her, and she couldn't possibly live up to that.

The doors slid open at the nineteenth floor and Shock took her elbow and guided her from the elevator. They walked down the hall and turned to the right, then stopped in front of a double door. He slid the key card into the slot and opened the door.

She stepped into the large suite and drew in a breath. There was a stunning view of the lakes out the window, the setting sun glinting on their golden surfaces, the sky alight with rose and mauve clouds outlined in golden sunlight.

The door closed behind them, and she felt Shock move closer. He put his arm around her waist and led her into the living room to the couch facing the window. They sat down, his arm still around her, and watched the sunset together. She noticed a standing bucket of ice with a bottle of champagne nestled in it.

"I'd like a glass of champagne," she said when he continued to ignore the bottle.

"Are you sure? After how it affected you earlier . . ."

She smiled. "It's not like you don't already have my consent, and . . . it will help me to relax."

He pulled the bottle from the bucket, popped the cork, and poured the sparkling wine into the tall stem glasses on the glass table in front of the couch, then handed her one.

"You're nervous."

She nodded, then clinked her glass against his. She went to drink and he stopped her, then hooked his arm around hers in a corny but romantic gesture. She sipped the champagne and felt the warmth flow down her throat, then spread through her whole body.

"You must know I won't hurt you."

"But . . ." She gazed at him with wide eyes. "What if I'm not all you hoped I'd be?"

He smiled tenderly and stroked the hair from her face. "There's absolutely no danger of that."

"But how do you know?"

"Because of who you are. Because of what we've already experienced." He drew her closer and brushed his lips against hers in a gentle caress. "Because of what I feel anytime I get near you."

He cupped the back of her head and drew her face closer, then kissed her again. This time deeper, and more poignantly.

"I want you so bad, every nerve in my body aches for you." He took her hand and pressed it to his chest, over his heart.

Under the fine silk of his shirt, Liv could feel his heart beating, a thunderous roar. She stared at his chest in wonder.

"Can you feel it? How much I want you?"

Could he mean he had deeper feelings for her, and wanted more than a physical relationship?

That thought shook her whole world.

Was he falling in love with her?

Because she could so easily fall head over heels in love with him.

She pulled the brakes on that line of thought. Shock had lusted after her for a long time and wanted to follow that attraction to its logical conclusion. That was all. Just a fling to experience what he couldn't in college.

The pounding of his heart was the result of physical desire. No more than that. And she would be a fool to believe there could be more.

He had waited a long time for this, so she wouldn't keep him waiting any longer.

She stood up and, heedless of the unobstructed window in front of them, and in the fiery finale of the blazing sunset, she pulled the straps of the black dress off her shoulders and allowed the slinky fabric to drop to the floor.

Shock had been watching her every move, and now his brown eyes heated to the color of dark chocolate as his gaze swept down her body, taking in every inch of her, then settling on her puckered nipples. She stepped toward him until her legs brushed against his knees, and he opened them and rested his hands on her waist, then drew her forward.

He admired her breasts, focusing on the hard nubs, then glanced at her face.

"You are incredibly sexy."

"The outfit you got me makes me look—"

He cut her off. "No. *You* are incredibly sexy. These things only enhance your incredible beauty."

She felt her cheeks flush. "Thank you."

He chuckled and tightened his hands around her waist, drawing her closer. "No, thank you."

Her breasts were at his eye level, and he stared at them, admiring. Finally, she reached around behind her and unfastened the hooks, then drew away the demi-bra, removing all barriers to his touch.

He took the hint and tucked his hand under one of her naked breasts, lifting slightly, then his thumb found the nub and brushed over it ever so lightly.

Sparks flared inside her.

"Oh, that feels so nice," she crooned.

He smiled and cupped the other breast, then brushed that nipple, too. She felt weak in the knees.

"Sit," he commanded, and when she did, he lowered himself to the floor, kneeling in front of her. He pressed her back against the couch, then leaned in and brushed his tongue lightly over her nipple.

"Oh, yes." She could barely handle the wave of subtle sensations sweeping through her like subdued fireworks expanding and flashing in slow motion.

After treating each of her nubs to his delicious tongue play, she felt his mouth close over one and suckle it ever so lightly. She melted against the back of the couch.

"Oh, God, that feels so good."

He caressed her other breast as he suckled her nipple, then he switched sides. She wove her fingers through his dark brown hair and found herself drawing him closer to her. He sucked harder and she gasped.

His hands glided downward, past the lacy garter belt at her waist, to the elastic of her tiny panties.

He smiled. "You put them on over the garter belt."

"Is that wrong?" she asked, drawn out of the web of pleasure.

He kissed her cheek. "No, it's perfect."

Then he pulled the delicate garment down her hips, and she lifted her ass so he could pull it down farther, then slide it off her legs.

He pressed her knees apart and stared at her intimate folds. She felt her cheeks heat. She loved his admiring gaze, but it made her self-conscious.

But he stroked her breast again, then his lips found her nipple and she floated away on a sea of sensual abandon.

His fingers glided down her belly and she tensed when she felt him stroke her folds, then glide along her slick slit. But he moved slowly and she soon found herself relaxing into the delightful sensations.

As he stroked her, an ache built deep inside that only he could fulfill. She clutched his shirt, needing more from him. But the feel of the smooth silk in her hands reminded her he was still fully clothed, while she was essentially naked.

She started unbuttoning his shirt, wanting to feel the warm, smooth skin of his broad chest. The heat inside her flared. She wanted to see his erection. To admire his extraordinarily long, thick member.

But he caught her hands, then raised them to his lips and kissed them. "Not yet, my love."

His mouth captured one of her nipples again and sucked, making her moan. Then he kissed lightly down her belly. She was caught up in the mesmerizing pleasure of his lips moving over her skin, but when she felt his fingers stroke her folds, and he pressed her knees wider and leaned in to kiss her down there, she gripped his shoulders and tried to draw him up again.

"No, I want you to make love to me. If you do that—"

"Liv, you know you can have more than one orgasm. If I give you pleasure now, you'll still be able to orgasm when we make love. Women have an infinite capacity for pleasure."

"It won't take away from . . . when we do it?"

He laughed and kissed her belly button. "Not at all. In fact, I think it will help relax you."

She stopped resisting as he spread her knees wide. His face moved lower, then she felt his tongue brush against her intimate flesh and she moaned.

"You are so sweet, my love. I could taste you all day long."

She arched against him and he pressed his tongue deeper inside her. His fingers drew her folds apart and his tongue drifted over her sensitive nub. She gasped at the exquisite pleasure.

"Oh, Shock." The pleasure increased. "Oh, yes."

His fingers played over her folds, dipping lightly into her opening as his tongue caressed and cajoled. She ran her fingers through his hair as he lapped at her, her breath quickening as more blissful sensations washed through her. His tongue swept over her clit again and she gasped. Then his fingers stroked her slit in sweeping motions, and she arched, moaning as intense pleasure swept through her like a tidal wave. She rode the crest of pleasure, moaning in ecstasy, her head thrown back.

It went on and on as he kept licking and stroking her in a never-ending flood of bliss.

Finally it ended in a slow descent from heaven, and she basked in the delight of his physical closeness.

He leaned back, a smile on his face. She gazed at him, a smile raising the corners of her own lips.

"I want to see you now. All of you," she said.

He stood up, his smile broadening, and he slowly stripped off his suit jacket, then his tie. He unbuttoned his shirt, one button at a time, whereas she would have wanted to tear them off in one jerk. She licked her lips as he pulled down his zipper, then pushed his pants past his hips. Then he stood before her with only black briefs on, not the boxers she knew he usually wore.

They were tight and sexy, showing the outline of his long, hard erection. In fact, the head started peeking out the top as she stared at him.

"You're so big."

He chuckled. "The better to fuck you with, my dear." Then his face grew somber. "I'm sorry, Liv. Are you worried? About my size, I mean? It might hurt a little, but it will pass."

"No, I like how big it is. It looks so . . . sturdy."

"I guess that's one way to describe it."

"Let's get it out here where I can see it so I can think of a better word."

He laughed and pushed his briefs to the ground, then stood up.

Her gaze fell on him and her insides quivered. She had seen him yesterday in the bathroom, but now he was totally naked, so she finally had a better appreciation of his length and girth.

Would that thing really fit inside her?

Her insides quivered. She hoped so!

"So, what do you have to say now?" he asked.

Her wide eyes stared at him for a while longer, an ache growing inside her. His cock twitched under her intense scrutiny.

"Awesome!"

He laughed.

Then she wrapped her hand around him and stroked.

"Come closer. I want it in my mouth."

He moved closer and she guided him to her lips and opened. Wide. His big, bulbous head slipped into her mouth and she wrapped her lips around him, licking the tip. Then she remembered that he'd told her he liked to be licked around the ridge of the head, so she ran her tongue around its underside.

"Oh, baby."

Then she sucked and he moaned. She stroked his balls, cupping and caressing them in her palm. She began to move up and down on his shaft, taking him as deep as she could, then gliding back, then going deep again. She continued to stroke him, and when she only had the head in her mouth, she began to suck.

"Baby, I'm not like you. If you make me come right now, I won't be able to make love to you, at least not right away."

He guided her away from his cock and locked gazes with her. "It's your choice, but if you finish this now, you'll have to wait before you can have the complete experience."

She was torn. She wanted to run her lips up and down his big cock and feel the pleasure of making him come. Feeling that power over him was a heady experience.

But her insides ached for the feel of him inside her. To have him glide deep into her, over and over again, until they both found their release together.

She leaned forward and kissed the tip of his cock, giving his shaft a little squeeze with her hand, then she let go and looked up at him.

"I want you to take me. Show me what it should be like between a man and a woman."

He smiled, then swept her into his arms and carried her into the bedroom. Liv gasped at the sight of a hundred pillar candles glowing around the room.

"Oh, it's beautiful. Why didn't you bring me in here right away?"

"Because it wouldn't have been as effective before the sun set."

She glanced around and realized the sun had gone down enough that it was getting dark.

Shock carried her to the bed and she saw that the covers had been turned down and red rose petals covered the white sheets. He laid her on the bed, then lay on his side beside her. His lips found hers and he kissed her. The scent of the petals, along with his musky male cologne, blended to an intoxicating fragrance. She breathed in deeply as she gazed into his eyes.

He stroked her hair from her face. "Are you ready, sweetheart?"

"Yes. Please make love to me, Shock. I want to feel you inside me."

He shifted over her, his knees between hers, then she felt something hot and hard press against her slick folds. His cockhead glided the length of her slit, then pressed against her center. She felt pressure as he pushed forward, slowly but steadily. His cockhead pushed inside a little, stretching her. A man had done this once before, so she knew she wouldn't have the pain of her hymen breaking again, but Shock was so big. So thick.

She started to get nervous and Shock must have seen it in her eyes. He kissed her lips. "Do you want me to stop?"

She hesitated, then shook her head. "No, I want this. Please, just push inside."

His cock glided forward in a slow steady stroke, pushing deep inside her. At first she felt pain, but as she grew accustomed to him, the discomfort gave way to pleasure. She clung to his shoulders, breathing heavily.

"Are you okay?" Shock asked against her ear.

She nodded, then found her voice. "Yes, I . . ." But there were no words to express the intensity of what she felt.

He drew back and she was afraid he was going to stop, but then he pushed into her again, slowly and gently.

As he pulled back again, his cockhead dragging along her inner passage, she moaned as her body grew more comfortable with him inside her. She'd never felt anything like this before. Exquisite. Delightful. Powerfully intense.

"Baby, I've wanted this for so long, I don't know how long I can hold on, but I'll try to keep going until you come. If I can't, I promise, I'll make it up to you," he said as he stroked inside her again.

"Just make love to me, Shock. That's all I need. No matter what happens."

He glided in and out of her, and pleasure swept through her. She clutched his shoulders and spread her legs wider, amazed at how her body had stretched to accommodate him.

"Oh, Shock, yes. It feels so good."

She wanted to burst into tears as he began to move faster, although she could tell by the tension in his muscles and his jaw that he was holding back, being gentle with her. Then a sudden burst of pleasure shot through her and she moaned.

Bliss continued to radiate through her, and she clung to his shoulders, moaning his name.

"Are you coming for me, baby?" he asked, staring into her eyes and pressing his forehead to hers.

She couldn't answer with the intense wave of sensations sweeping over her, but she murmured his name again and again. Then she felt him jerk forward, and she could feel his cock pulsing inside her, hot liquid filling her. The sensation had a magical effect on her, driving her over the edge and catapulting her to a mind-shattering orgasm.

She held on tight to Shock as they both moaned their releases.

He kept driving into her, keeping her in a state of ecstasy for what seemed like forever.

But finally he slowed and she floated back to earth.

"Baby, that was fantastic," he panted against her ear. He kissed her, then smiled. "I got the feeling you enjoyed it, too."

She shrugged and tried to hold back a smile. "It was okay."

He raised an eyebrow in response, and she buried her head against his chest and laughed. She never knew sex would be so much fun.

She relaxed into his arms and just enjoyed the afterglow. Soon she felt herself drift off in the warmth of his embrace.

Liv woke up in the middle of the night in the comfort of Shock's arms, and she realized she wanted to be there forever. For him it might just be a physical relationship, something he'd longed to experience with her since college, but to her it was much, much more.

He had awakened her sensuality again. He was someone she could trust, despite the contract and the rocky start.

But it was deeper than that. There were underlying feelings she couldn't ignore.

Damn it, she should have known better than to allow this to happen between them, because she was falling in love with him.

Totally. And completely. In love.

She sucked in a breath as she listened to his heart beat against her ear.

She loved him.

She stroked his chest, enjoying the closeness of their bodies, but she realized that was all it was. Physical intimacy.

He wanted to fuck her. For a month.

Then it would end.

Shock sensed something had changed. The next morning when they woke up, Liv was still in his arms, and still needy and wanting when he kissed her. They made love with the same intense passion as last night.

But afterward there was some distance between them.

They showered and dressed. He'd arranged to have casual clothes for both of them brought to the hotel, so they didn't have to leave in the same clothes they'd worn last night, even though he'd definitely love to see her in that dress again.

The limo pulled up in front of his country house and for a moment he regretted bringing her back here, where he wouldn't have her all to himself.

Of course, he would sexually. She'd made it clear she didn't want to have sex with other men, so she wouldn't be like Raven and Tempest and share her favors among the crew.

And he was glad. He was thankful that Rip and Steele were so generous with their women, and that their women were so willing, but now that he'd been with Liv, he wanted her all to himself.

Luckily, she wanted the same thing.

He opened the door and they went inside. The house was quiet, even though all the bikes were outside.

"They're probably all out at the pool or in the lake. Let's go upstairs and get settled."

She nodded and they went up the wide staircase together. Once in the room, he considered pulling her into his arms and ravaging her all over again, but she walked to the big window.

"This is actually a door to outside," she said. "I didn't know there was a balcony out there."

As soon as she slid the door open, he heard it. Moaning. Two people—no, more—having sex.

He raced to the door, intent on pulling her back. She wasn't ready to see that. It would probably intimidate her. Make her worry he would demand that of her, since he'd included it in the sexual contract, to push her. Damn it, he'd have to talk to her about that. Ensure she really knew that he didn't expect anything like that of her.

But she was out the door before he could stop her.

As he reached her side, her eyes widened as she gazed down over the balcony railing.

"Oh, my God," she murmured.

He glanced over the railing. First he saw Dom sitting on the side of the pool with a totally naked Raven sucking his big cock while Magic watched. Tempest, also naked, was sitting on Wild Card's lap, his hands cupping her breasts while Rip gave her oral sex. Steele watched them, stroking his own cock.

"Fuck, bitch, suck me harder," Dom demanded.

Shock cringed. That was just Dom. He used coarse language during sex, but Raven loved it. He glanced at Liv, worried it would frighten her and set her back in the progress she'd made.

She watched them intently.

"Come on, Liv. Let's go inside. You shouldn't be seeing this."

Her gaze raised to his and locked on. He almost thought he saw heat in her eyes, instead of the disgust or anxiety he was sure she was feeling.

"No, I want to watch," she said, sending a jolt of surprise through him.

Liv was mesmerized by the sight of the naked bodies twined in sexual abandon, and the sounds of their pleasure aroused her. In fact, she wished she had the guts to go down there and take part.

The contract with Shock mentioned all kinds of sexual things to do, including him sharing her with other men. Being with Shock had been her first step to regaining her confidence with respect to sex, so maybe she should take advantage of the situation to expand her experience to include other men. She knew she'd be safe with Shock and his friends. Shock wouldn't let anyone hurt her.

But she wasn't ready.

Watching was exciting, though. It made her feel wicked, and it turned her on immensely. She slid in front of Shock and took his hands, then pressed them to her breasts. He cupped her, squeezing her soft mounds in his big hands.

She watched as Magic stepped behind Raven and pressed his stiff cock against her. Slowly, he glided into her from behind. Tempest moaned and arched against Rip's mouth as Wild Card caressed her breasts. She threw her head back and moaned loudly as Rip drove her to orgasm. He drew away, then stood up and grasped his cock, pressed it to her slick opening, then drove inside her. Within minutes she was moaning again.

Raven began to moan, too, and Liv shifted to watch Magic thrusting into her.

Liv's insides melted, longing to feel what Raven and Tempest were feeling. If only she had the courage.

God, they were so comfortable with their sexuality.

Shock nuzzled her ear. "Is this turning you on, sweetheart?"

She nodded, pressing his hands tighter to her breasts.

Tempest now leaned against the side of the pool and Wild Card stepped behind her. He pressed his cock to her ass, then slowly glided forward. *Oh, God, he was taking her from behind.* The thought sent shivers through her.

"That must hurt," Liv said.

"If the man knows what he's doing, and is patient, it is extremely pleasurable for the woman." He smiled. "Or so Raven and Tempest tell me."

Once Wild Card was all the way inside her, he turned them both and rested against the side of the pool, then Steele stepped toward her, a big smile on his face and his cock at full mast.

"Oh, God, is he going to . . ." Her words trailed off as Steele pressed his cock to her slit and pushed inside her.

Shock's hand glided down her stomach, then held her firmly against him. His cock was fully erect, pressing against her.

"Both of them are inside her at the same time," she said in awe.

She undulated against him, longing for his big shaft inside her.

Shock tugged at the hem of her T-shirt and pulled it over her head, then his hands cupped her breasts again.

Below, Raven was bent over and sucking Dom's huge cock while Magic fucked her from behind. Tempest was leaning back against Wild Card, his cock inside her ass while Steele drove his big cock into her again and again. Liv's breathing increased at the erotic sight.

She felt Shock's fingers working at her jeans, then the snap released and he pulled down her zipper. His fingers slid under the denim, then inside her panties. When she felt his fingertips glide over her folds, she moaned softly, her gaze locked on Steele's hard ass as it clenched and he groaned against Tempest. Tempest was already moaning in climax.

Then Shock's fingers slid inside her and her eyelids closed.

"Oh, that feels so good."

"You're so wet. God, I want to be inside you."

She turned in his arms and his mouth covered hers. She slid her hands under his shirt and stroked his hard, sculpted chest.

He swept her up in his arms and carried her into the bedroom, then set her down on the bed. He pulled her jeans off and tossed then aside, then he peeled away his shirt and stripped off his jeans. The whole time his hot gaze was focused on her in her lacy bra and panties. Her breathing accelerated as he pushed down his boxers, revealing his hard cock, the veins pulsing along the shaft.

Primal moans from outside filled her with heat, reminding her of the naked bodies writhing together downstairs. Of multiple men filling each woman.

Her blood boiled as Shock approached the bed. She unfastened her bra and tossed it aside. Both their hands reached her panties at the same time and Shock stripped them away in one motion. He sat on the bed beside her and caressed her breasts, then trailed his hand down her stomach to her damp folds. She opened her legs in invitation and he slid two fingers inside her and stroked her inner passage, leaning over and capturing her lips. His tongue pulsed into her mouth as his fingers did the same between her legs. She arched against his hand.

"Oh, Shock. I need you," she cried. "Please fill me. Now."

He chuckled and prowled over her. He pressed his cock to her opening, then glided inside. She moaned at the feel of his thick shaft entering her, unrelenting, all the way to the hilt. When he was all the way inside, she clutched him tightly to her, both of them breathing hard, overwhelmed by the feeling of him inside her. The two of them joined as one.

She wanted to feel this intimacy with him forever.

He nuzzled her neck. "You feel so good around me, sweetheart. I could stay like this forever."

Joy burst through her at his tender words.

She wrapped her legs around him and arched upward, wanting him deeper still. He groaned, then started to move. His big shaft glided along her passage, stroking the intimate flesh, then pushed deep again. She squeezed as it slid out and in again, to his moan of pleasure.

He sped up, gliding faster, until he was filling her with deep, hard strokes. She moaned against his ear, pleasure rising with each thrust of his body.

She began to tremble, clinging to his shoulders. Arching against his body. Until an intense wave of joy swept through her.

"Yes, Shock. Oh, God, yes."

The next thrust flung her to ecstatic heights, and she wailed her release.

Shock groaned and ground his pelvis against her. Her intimate muscles clenched around his pulsing cock, then she felt the heat of him releasing inside her.

They both collapsed, gasping for air. Shock's big body was on top of her, the bulk of his weight on his arms. When he started to move away, she tightened her arms around him.

"Don't go yet," she murmured, then dragged her teeth over the coarse whiskers on his jaw.

"I'm heavy."

"I don't mind."

He lay there for a few minutes, his lips playing along her temple. So soft and tender. Finally, he rolled to his side, holding her against his hard torso, his arms around her. She rested her head against his chest and smiled. If she had her choice, this was where she would stay for the rest of her life.

Liv followed Shock into the dimly lit roadhouse and sat down at the big wooden table with the others. After joining the crew on the main floor, they'd all gone out for a ride on their bikes, then decided to stop here to eat.

The waitress brought them beers and they all ordered the house burger. As they relaxed and enjoyed the meal, Liv watched the others together and admired their easy camaraderie. She wished she could be a part of this group for real, but her time here would end too soon. And when that ended, she would probably never see Shock again.

"Hey, what's wrong?" Raven, who was sitting next to Liv, asked. She spoke quietly, not drawing attention from the lively discussion around the table.

"Nothing," Liv said, gazing uncomfortably at the other woman. "Why?"

Raven shrugged. "Well, for someone who just had great sex, you seem pretty tense."

"Why do you think that . . ." But Liv trailed off and shook her head. There was no way she could convince the woman she and Shock hadn't had sex, so she said the only thing she could think of. "That it was great?"

"Come on. It's clear you're both totally hot for each other, and you two took off last night, I assume to have some long, leisurely time together." She grinned. "And don't forget, I've been with the man." But then her smile faded. "Unless that's it. Wasn't it great? Are you two having problems?"

"No," Liv said quickly, then sighed. "It was totally great. He's great. But . . ."

She shrugged. What could she say? That the only reason she was here was because she'd signed a contract to be Shock's sex slave for a month because he'd loaned her money?

Or did Raven already know? Did all of them know?

"But what?" Raven asked.

"Nothing. We're just . . . getting used to each other, I guess."

"I thought you guys have known each other since college."

Liv nodded, not quite sure what Shock had told the others about her. "We have. But . . . what has he told you about us?"

Raven shrugged. "Not much. Just that you were friends. I don't know how close, but I got the impression he'd like to be closer. A lot closer."

Liv nodded again. "This . . . sexual thing between us . . . is new."

"I get it. You're still getting to know each other that way." She rested her hand on Liv's arm. "But, honey, you seem so stressed. If you want to talk about it . . ."

Liv glanced at Shock, who had glanced her way once or twice while she and Raven talked but still kept his conversation going with the others.

Liv was sure he wouldn't like her revealing their secrets to anyone else.

She shook her head. "I'm okay. But thanks."

Raven nodded. "Okay, but if you change your mind, I'm here."

Liv sipped her beer, not sure what to do with the friendly offer Raven had made. Liv hadn't opened up to another female since her last year of college, when she'd closed herself off to everyone. She hadn't even confided in her sister. Not about her relationships anyway.

Who was she kidding? She'd never really had a relationship. She'd been too afraid to let anyone get close. And she'd never wanted to tell anyone what had happened to her. Not even her sister.

How stupid she'd been.

So not only had that bastard stolen her ability to have a normal relationship with a man, he'd caused her to deny herself close, meaningful friendships with women, too.

Anger seared through her and she sipped her beer again. Then gulped it. When it was gone, she signaled the waitress for another.

"That's your fourth," Shock said a little while later.

She glared at him. "So what? Why do you care how much I drink?"

He frowned, his gaze gliding over her face. He grasped her arm and stood up. "We're leaving."

"What if I don't want to go?" she demanded.

Everyone stared at her, and suddenly she felt like a spoiled brat demanding her own way. Slowly, she stood up and let him lead her to the door.

Once they stepped out into the cool night, and Liv

took a deep breath of fresh air, her knees grew wobbly. Shock tightened his arm around her and steadied her.

"What did Raven say that upset you?"

"Raven didn't upset me."

He watched her as they walked to his bike. "You could have fooled me." He grabbed a helmet and put it on her head, then fastened the strap under her chin. "Then what put you in such a bad mood?"

"I'm not in a bad mood." But she could hear the defiant note in her voice and couldn't even convince herself of that.

There was no reason to take it out on Shock. "I'm sorry. She asked if everything was okay between us and I didn't know what to say."

"Isn't everything okay between us?"

She shrugged. "I don't know. I don't know what this is. I'm not sure how to behave." She gazed up at him. "Other than when we're together, doing whatever you say."

"Does that bother you?"

"It's not that. It's just . . . I don't know how to react to your friends' questions . . . or what to tell them about us."

"Did Raven question you about what's going on between us?"

"No. Not specifically. She was just . . . really nice. She seemed to care because she thinks we're having problems."

"Of course she cares. She's a good friend."

Liv pursed her lips and nodded. "I just . . . I don't know what to do with that."

He stroked his hand along her back. "Why do I get

the impression that you don't really know what it's like to have a close friend?"

To her horror, Liv felt tears prickling at her eyes. Shock ran his thumb under her eye, wiping a droplet aside.

"Fuck, Liv." Then he pulled her into his arms and held her.

It would be so easy to let go. To let the tears flow and sob in his warm, protective embrace.

But she didn't. She stiffened and blinked back the tears.

After a moment, he drew back and gazed at her. Then he sucked in a breath and climbed onto the bike. She joined him and hung on tight as they drove into the night.

When they arrived back at the house, Liv got off the bike and handed Shock her helmet, then went in the front door, not waiting for him.

Now they were going to go to the bedroom where he would make love to her. Her heart raced at the thought, longing to be in his arms. Or he would forgo sex and just cuddle her close, being understanding because he knew she was upset. Which made her heart ache.

She couldn't do this. Let herself want him so much.

Instead of heading for the stairs, she walked into the kitchen. Through the big windows, she could see the freeform-shaped pool edged with violet, blue, and red colored lights, setting it aglow. Colored mosaic stained-glass globes lit the granite pathways leading from the house to the pool to the hot tub and to the lovely sitting area beyond. Farther away, moonlight glittered on the lake.

She opened the French doors and stepped onto the patio.

"What are you doing, Liv?" Shock asked behind her.

"I think I'll go for a swim."

"Without your swimsuit?" he asked.

She glanced back at him. "Do I need one?"

She unbuckled her jeans and dropped them to the ground.

Shock smiled. "Not as far as I'm concerned."

She pulled her T-shirt over her head as she continued walking through the dimly lit yard. Then she shed her bra. Shock followed her, shedding his shirt and jeans, too. Leaving on her panties, she sped up as she approached the pool and dove in. When she surfaced, she shook her head and glanced around.

"Uh . . . just wanted to let you know I'm here." Wild Card's voice caught her off guard.

He was hard to see in the softly lit pool, sitting on the walk-out steps at the deep end with a beer on the stone deck beside him. She'd forgotten that Wild Card had decided not to go out with them this evening.

She realized she was practically naked in the pool with him, and Shock was standing on the edge of the pool behind her in his boxers.

Part of her wanted to cover herself and swim away, then skulk out of the pool and hide. Another part thought this was a perfect opportunity to distract herself from her desire for Shock and start convincing herself that other men could fill that need. After seeing them all together earlier and being surprised by how arousing she found it, she wondered if Shock was right to encourage her to push herself sexually. And it would have the added benefit of easing her heartache about him.

She swam toward Wild Card, then treaded water in front of him. The soft colored lights set her naked breasts aglow. Wild Card gazed at them with admiration.

"What are you doing, Liv?" Shock said with a warning tone.

"You told me that you all share your women." She smiled at Wild Card. "I thought that might be fun to try tonight."

She swam close to Wild Card and rested her hands on his thighs so she could stop treading water. "What do you think?" she asked him.

He glanced up at Shock, so she moved into Wild Card's arms and kissed him, not wanting to give Shock a chance to protest. Wild Card's arms slid around her and he pulled her close, her naked breasts crushed against his hard chest.

She teased his lips with her tongue and he opened them, then slipped his tongue into her mouth. With one hand on the side of the pool and the other arm around her waist, he slid off the stairs and turned her around. When he pressed her tight to the wall of the pool, his rock-hard erection pressed against her, and she gasped.

Panic tore through her. This wasn't what she wanted.

He was strong and powerful. And scary.

She sucked in a breath and pushed him back.

He moved away easily and gazed at her, his eyes questioning. "What is it, Liv?" he asked.

"This was a mistake. I . . ." But she just shook her head and swam across the pool. Straight to Shock.

He reached down and she took his hand, letting him pull her from the water, then tuck his arm around her waist. She peered over her shoulder as Shock guided her back toward the house.

"I'm sorry, Wild Card."

"It's okay. Maybe another time."

Shock didn't even stop to pick up her clothes, just hurried her up the stairs and into the bedroom.

"What were you thinking?" he demanded as soon as the door closed behind them.

She went straight into the bathroom and grabbed a towel to dry off, not wanting to listen to his lecture, but he followed her in.

"I just wanted to try being with someone else." She hated that her voice trembled. "You suggested it in the contract, so I don't know why you're getting upset."

"I didn't say I'm upset, but clearly you aren't ready for that."

"So I just need more time, is that what you're saying? Then I can be a slut and sleep with all your friends."

He frowned. "If you think it's a negative thing being with Wild Card, why did you want to do it?"

"I don't think that. I . . ." She sighed in frustration. "I'm just . . . confused."

"I think you're just trying to get back at me."

"For what?"

"I don't know. Forcing you into this situation with the contract."

She shook her head, but said nothing.

"Then maybe you're just trying to push me away," he said.

"Why would I do that?"

"I don't know. Maybe because you're starting to develop feelings for me?"

His words were like a bucket of cold water splashed across her. Oh, God, she couldn't let him know that was true. And she didn't want to get pulled any deeper into her well of emotions.

Even if it would be good for her to end this now, she didn't want it to end one second sooner than it had to.

"No, you don't have to worry about that," she said. "I know exactly what this is."

He raised an eyebrow. "And what is it?"

"Me meeting your physical needs for one month. You've always wanted to explore the physical attraction between us, and that's what this is. Then, when I'm out of your system at the end of the month, it ends."

He narrowed his eyes. "And you don't want it to be any more than that?"

She gazed at him, keeping her heart in check. "No. Of course not."

Shock's chest tightened. So she was only doing this to meet the requirements of the loan. She didn't feel anything for him.

The rejection hurt. She'd rejected him before, but this time, he'd hoped she would feel something for him.

Maybe even fall in love with him.

"If you're so keen to follow the contract, then let's start with you being my slave and obeying my every whim."

At the hard edge to his voice, her eyes widened.

"Strip off those panties and get down on your knees."

"But—"

"Obey me immediately," he demanded in an iron tone, "and with no argument."

When she still hesitated, he stepped toward her. "Now!"

She tugged off her panties and dropped to her knees.

"Eyes to the floor."

She dropped her gaze to the cold white tiles.

"Good. Now you will do everything I tell you, without question. And when you respond to me, you will call me 'Sir.' Do you understand?"

"Yes, Sir."

Her voice quivered, and he felt a little guilty, but he pushed it aside. She was rash and had gotten herself into trouble. She could use the discipline.

"Stand up and walk into the bedroom."

He followed her, then gestured to the love seat.

"Sit."

She walked to the love seat and sat down, watching him with her wide blue eyes.

"Now spread your legs."

She obeyed, spreading her knees wide.

Having her completely at his mercy caused his cock to lengthen. And the sight of her sweet pussy open to him made his heart race. He wanted to touch her. To push inside her.

But even more, right now he wanted to see her touch her soft, intimate flesh.

He sat down in the chair across from her, his attention fixed on her pink folds.

"Now touch yourself."

She frowned as she gazed up at him, then seemed to remember his command to keep her eyes lowered and dropped her gaze again. She moved her hand slowly, pressing her fingers between her legs, and started to stroke her folds.

Fuck, it was so sexy, his cock began to throb. She stroked along her slit, back and forth.

"Dip your fingers inside." He watched as the tips of her fingers disappeared, then more as she continued up to her knuckles.

"Are you wet?" he asked.

"Yes, Sir."

He moved forward and dropped to his knees in front of her, watching her fingers, wanting his own fingers inside her.

"Does it feel good touching yourself?"

She glanced up at him again, frowning. "I . . . I'd rather it was you."

He smiled. "Soon. Right now I like watching you."

Then he caught her wrist and drew her hand forward. He wrapped his lips around her fingers and sucked. The sweet taste of her sent his hormones into overdrive.

"You taste so fucking good."

"Thank you, Sir."

He sat on the love seat beside her.

"Come and touch me now."

She moved onto her knees in front of him. At first she ran her hands over his shoulders, then across his chest.

Her fingertips found his nipples and she toyed with them, sending heat simmering through him. He wanted to feel her lips on him. She began to move her hands down his chest, but he captured them and brought them back to his nipples.

"Don't rush away so fast."

She glanced at his face questioningly, then at his nipples, which were hard as beads. She ran her fingertips over them, noticing the catch in his breath. Then she leaned forward and licked one, then took the little bead in her mouth, and began to suck.

"Oh, fuck, yeah, Liv."

She sucked harder and he groaned.

He took her hand and pressed it to his cock. She wrapped her fingers around it, through the thin fabric of his boxers, and squeezed, making him groan again. When she began to stroke him up and down, he knew this would end too quickly.

He stood up and walked to his dresser, then opened the drawer and pulled out a pair of handcuffs.

Her gaze locked on them as he returned to her.

He would take this opportunity to show her that she could give total control to a man, and if he cared for her, he would be devoted to her pleasure. Not like that bastard who had hurt her.

"Get on the bed."

She stood up and walked to the bed, then stretched out on it. He snapped a cuff around one of her wrists, threaded the chain around an intricately carved section of the wrought-iron headboard, then cuffed her other wrist.

Then he stepped back, taking in the glorious sight of her stretched out on the bed before him.

"Open your legs."

She obeyed, her cheeks flushing. He stepped to the side of the bed, stroking his hard, aching cock.

"Now suck me." He pressed his cockhead against her cheek.

"Yes, Sir."

She turned toward him and he directed his cock toward her mouth. When her lips parted, he glided his tip inside.

"Now, slave, suck hard," he demanded.

It was so hot and moist in her mouth, he twitched in need. Heat pulsed through him.

"I'm close. Make me come."

She bobbed up and down, then sucked the tip of him hard, then bobbed again. Her hot mouth sent pleasure rocking through him.

"Fuck, that's so good."

Then she squeezed him inside and pleasure blasted through him, his pelvis rocked forward, and he erupted in her mouth. She kept sucking as he flooded into her, filling her mouth with his hot seed.

When he finished, she continued to suck softly, then licked around his cockhead before she released him and drew her mouth away.

He could get used to this. Her obeying his commands. Not challenging him.

He sat on the bed beside her and stroked her breasts lightly with his fingertips. Her nipples peaked into tight buds. He leaned down and suckled one in his mouth, to her soft whimpers of appreciation.

He slid his hand down her stomach, and lightly caressed her between her thighs and along her slick slit. She whimpered louder. He brushed his lips against her hip as he continued to slide his fingers along her folds.

"Open wider."

She spread her legs wider and he gazed at the wet, intimate flesh in front of him. His cock, although emptied, twitched at the sight. He leaned down and licked her.

"Oh, yes," she moaned.

He climbed onto the bed and knelt between her legs, then licked her slit again. Then he drove his tongue into her. Her soft moans encouraged him.

He opened her folds and slipped a finger inside her, then another. As he gently thrust into her, he found her clit with his other hand and stroked it.

"Ohhh." She lifted her hips higher.

Shock continued to thrust and tease. Her moans increased. He teased her little button faster and she whimpered, then moaned louder.

He wanted to see her face in sweet rapture. He looked up at her, burying his tongue in her hot flesh and licking her clit.

Then she gasped and moaned her release, long and loud. The sound of her pleasure vibrated through him, giving him intense pleasure, too.

As her orgasm subsided, he climbed all the way onto the bed and covered her body with his.

His cock was hard with need and he pressed it against her, teasing her sensitized clit, eliciting more muffled sounds of pleasure. Then he drove into her, loving the sound of her gasp and of the way her eyes widened.

"Do you like me inside you?" he asked.

"Yes, Sir."

Fuck, the sound of her calling him "Sir," especially with his cock sunk deep inside her, sent need pulsing through him. He drew back and surged deep again. Her eyes widened as he swirled around inside her.

Then he stopped.

"Do you want me to fuck you?" he asked.

She gazed up at him and nodded.

He pressed harder into her.

"Tell me," he demanded.

"Please fuck me, Sir."

He smiled and drew back, then drove deep again. She was so soft and warm around him. Her body so accepting of his.

"Tell me more. Why do you want me to fuck you?"

He wanted to hear how much she needed him.

"Yes, Sir. I want you. Your cock filling me . . . it makes me feel good."

He thrust deep again, then drew back until he was almost at the point of pulling out entirely. "Do you need me inside you?"

"Yes." She wrapped her legs around him and arched, trying to force him farther inside, but he drew back a little, teasing her. "It feels so good when you're deep inside me. Please, I need you."

Fuck, those were the words he wanted to hear. That she needed him. He'd always wanted to hear them.

He drove forward, filling her to the hilt, then pulled

back and thrust again, then kept on thrusting until her moans turned to wails and she gasped and cried out in ecstasy.

She tightened her legs around him as she found her release in his arms, and he erupted inside her, joining her in a joint journey to total fulfillment.

A few moments later, he realized he was lying on top of her with his full weight and she probably couldn't breathe. He rolled away and unfastened the cuffs, then pulled her into his arms. She snuggled against his chest and he sighed, enjoying the feel of her within the confines of his embrace.

Soon her even breathing told him she was asleep. He stroked her hair, loving her so close to him.

Loving her.

God, he had to find a way to convince her she loved him just as much as he loved her, because he knew, with everything he was, that he would not be able to let go of her at the end of the month.

Liv woke up in Shock's strong arms, the steady rhythm of his heartbeat in her ear.

She could get used to this. Waking up in his arms.

Last night had been . . . surprising. She never thought she'd enjoy being ordered around by a man, but with Shock it was pure pleasure. For some reason, she responded easily to his control, at least in the bedroom. It wasn't like when he lectured her or was disapproving of her actions. When he commanded her in the bedroom, she could just give herself over to him and their shared pleasure.

Because she trusted him. In fact, she realized he was the only person in the world she truly did trust.

His lips brushed against the back of her neck and his arms tightened around her.

"Did you sleep well?" he asked, his voice husky from sleep.

"Yes, Sir."

She smiled as she felt his cock swell. She could tell last night that her calling him "Sir" was a real turn-on for him.

And it certainly was for her.

She turned in his arms to face him and he kissed her. Sweet and tenderly. When their lips parted, she smiled.

"Would you like me to make you breakfast, Sir?" she asked.

"No, you stay right here. I'll make you one of my special omelets." He brushed her hair from her face and kissed her. Then he rolled from the bed and stood up.

She watched him walk to the bathroom door, enjoying the sight of his tight, sexy butt. Then she lay back and stared at the ceiling, remembering how delightful it had been to follow his commands last night. She must have dozed off in the midst of her reverie, because when she opened her eyes, she realized Shock was gone.

Liv got out of bed and showered, then dried her hair and dressed. As she walked down the stairs, she could hear several voices, probably the others having breakfast.

She walked into the living room on her way to the kitchen and froze when she saw Wild Card. He was the only person in the room and sat in the armchair facing the window. When he turned toward her, she immediately dropped her gaze to the stars silhouetted by red, purple, and blue swirls tattooed on his arm. Her cheeks flamed as she remembered stripping practically naked in front of him, then throwing herself at him.

"Oh, good morning," she said.

He gazed at her with his warm hazel eyes and his initial smile faded as he realized she could barely look at him.

"Hey, you're not going to let it get all weird between us, are you?"

"I'm . . . really sorry about last night."

He stood up and walked toward her. "You *are* going to let it get weird." He took her hand. "Look, I loved it, okay? Come on. A naked woman kissing me?"

His infectious grin relaxed her a little. He wasn't judging her.

"I mean, sure," he teased, "her then choosing her boyfriend over me hurt a little, but I get it." He took her hand and squeezed it. "So, we good?"

She gazed into his hazel eyes and smiled timidly. "Yeah, of course."

"Liv, you coming for breakfast?"

She turned to see Shock standing in the kitchen doorway, watching them. His sharp gaze dropped to their joined hands and Liv immediately drew her hand from Wild Card's.

In the kitchen, Shock served her an omelet, toast, and coffee, and she sat with Steele and Tempest and shared small talk, conscious of Shock's silence. After breakfast, she helped Shock with the dishes, wondering if he was going to give her the silent treatment all day.

"I thought we'd do something special today," he said as he wiped his hands on a towel, the pots all clean in the dish drainer by the sink.

"Like what?" she asked, relieved he was speaking to her.

"There's a small island on the lake with a nice beach. I thought we might go over there, just the two of us. Take a picnic lunch."

She smiled. "That sounds nice."

Shock watched her as the light breeze caught her hair and it fluttered around her face as the canoe skimmed through the water. He steered and she paddled in front of him. A pair of loons swam a few yards from them and she turned her head to watch them. His heart thumped at the sight of her profile. Her pert, upturned nose, her lips, parted slightly, the crinkle around her eyes as she smiled at the feathery little creatures.

She was always so willful, so prone to putting herself into questionable situations, but he'd seen another side of her now. He'd seen the depth of her vulnerability. Yet her strength in spite of that vulnerability impressed him.

He would have never guessed what had happened to her in college. She was like the loons swimming near them. On the surface, they seemed calm, gliding through the water effortlessly, but beneath them their feet were moving in a mad, fluttering pace to maintain that façade.

Another loon called in the distance, a lonely, haunting sound.

What the hell had he been thinking, insisting she be his for a month?

But he couldn't help himself. He'd wanted her.

Hell, he'd wanted her more than he'd ever wanted anything in his life.

So when the opportunity presented itself, he'd jumped at it.

He steered the canoe around to the other side of the island. When they landed on the beach, he steadied the boat while she stepped onto the sand. He pulled out the cooler they had brought while she carried a couple of bags packed with stuff.

Shock spread a blanket on the sand and invited her to sit, then handed her a cold bottle of pink lemonade.

"This is nice," she said, looking out over the water.

Maybe he shouldn't have forced her to be here, but he wouldn't give up this time with her for anything.

She glanced at him, catching his gaze on her face. "What?"

"I was just thinking I'm glad you're here."

"On the island?"

"The whole thing."

"You mean you're glad I needed money and asked you for it?"

Hell, no. He wished she were here because she wanted to be with him.

"Sure," he answered. If she wanted to keep it flip, so would he. "Why did you borrow the money, anyway?"

Her gaze jolted to his. "I thought you were okay with not knowing."

"You can't blame me for being curious. It's quite a lot of money. I can't help wondering how you got yourself into such a huge mess that you needed that much. You have a good job, yet you don't even have a decent place to live . . . and you needed that much cash?" He shrugged again. "I know you're rash, but I just never thought you'd get yourself in that deep."

She shook her head, her eyes taking on a disturbing clarity. "You think I"—she shook her head—"what? Gambled? Lost a ton of money and owed someone? Or maybe you think I'm into drugs?" Her eyes flashed as she held up her bare arms, then ran her hand over each one as if to show there were no needle marks. "You really think I'm a stupid little bitch, don't you?"

He didn't let her anger throw him. She deserved to blow off some steam.

"No, I didn't think either of those things. Not about you."

She held her head up in defiance. "Then what did you think?"

"I didn't know what to think, but the fact is, you did need a lot of money. That means bad decisions made." He frowned. "Like maybe that guy I saw you with at the bar."

Her eyebrow arched. "The guy who tried to pick me up, then attacked us later? What would that have to do with the money I needed?"

"No, the other guy. The second night." He leaned toward her. "What happened, Liv? Were you in some kind of relationship with him? Did he con you out of money?"

She gazed at him and the pain in her face caught him off guard. That was it. She'd been in a relationship with that guy and he'd played her.

"Fuck, Liv. You always were more giving than you could afford. And you trust people too much."

Her eyes widened and the sheen warned him she was close to shedding tears. "I . . . trust . . . people . . . too . . . much?" she repeated, each word an effort for her to say. "So . . . you think what happened to me was my own fault."

"Getting into debt?" He was confused. Of course it was her fault.

But she shook her head and he suddenly realized what she was really asking.

His heart clenched. "No, Liv. I didn't mean that."

She turned and strode away from him, but not before he saw the glitter of tears streaking down her face. He rushed forward and caught her arm.

"Liv, I'm sorry," he said, turning her around to face him. "Of course I don't think that."

She glared at him, her expression fierce. "You've always criticized me for being too rash—lectured me that it would get me into trouble." She shrugged her arm from his hold and stepped back. "And you were right, weren't you? I'm still getting into trouble." She dropped her head, staring at the ground. "That's how I wound up here."

With him. She didn't say it, but it was what she meant.

"I don't want you to be in trouble, Liv. Nothing about you being in pain makes me happy." He reached for her but she took another step backward, keeping a distance between them. "That's why I helped you. Liv, I'll always be there to help you."

• • •

Liv stared at him, blinking back the tears she didn't want to shed, even though some had already escaped. She couldn't hide them from him, but she could at least try to maintain a level of dignity and strength.

"I don't need you to be there."

God, she sounded ungrateful. She wrapped her arms around herself, feeling way too vulnerable.

"I mean"—she swatted away the tears pushing from her eyes—"I appreciate what you've done. And I will pay you back. But then I'll rely on myself."

This time he was able to capture her hand before she could escape, and she offered no resistance as he held it in his.

"I know, Liv. And you'll do an amazing job. I just wanted you to know you could call on me if you want."

Then he pulled her into his arms and held her close. Wanting to protect her. From life. From all the bad things around her.

From herself and her fierce desire to stand on her own and to face the worst in life even when help was standing right beside her.

Her resistance seeped away, and she melted against him, her head resting against his chest. He rested his chin on top of her head, her soft hair wisping around his chin with the breeze.

He could stand here forever, just holding her like this.

Liv helped Shock carry the stuff back from the canoe to the house. She had enjoyed the picnic on the island, relaxing with Shock, enjoying the sunshine, the sound of the water, and just being with him.

"I have to go into town for a meeting this afternoon," Shock said.

"Oh, what kind of meeting?"

"The company I use to manage the property we're staying at and the law firm I use for a lot of my business dealings are in town. Anytime I'm here, I arrange to go in and meet with them." He raised an eyebrow. "Do you want to come with me? I'll be busy for a few hours, but you could do some exploring, then we can meet for dinner. There's a great restaurant overlooking the lake."

"That sounds really nice. Should I change into something different?" But she wasn't sure what that would be. All she had were the biker chick clothes Shock had arranged for her, and the fancy dress she'd worn out to dinner, but that wasn't really appropriate for wandering around a small town in the afternoon.

"No, you're fine. I'm going in this," he said, gesturing to his worn jeans and T-shirt.

He picked up her leather jacket and held it for her. She slipped her arms in the sleeves and zipped it up as he pulled on his own jacket. Soon she was sitting behind him on his Harley as they zipped along the highway into town.

It didn't take long to get there, and as they rode along the main street, she glanced around at the quaint buildings. It was a lovely town, with lots of outdoor cafés, planters full of flowers along the wide sidewalks, and colorful banners fluttering in the breeze. Shock pulled over to the side of the road in front of a tall brown-brick building.

"It's a pretty town," she said as she pulled off her helmet.

"I like it," he said, as he took her helmet and stowed it in the saddle bag on his bike.

"There's a crafts market on the next street," he said, pointing to the right, "a park a couple of blocks further down, right off the lake and, of course, you can see a lot of restaurants along Main Street if you want something."

He pulled his wallet from his pocket and took out some bills, then handed them to her.

She frowned and shook her head.

He took her hand and pressed the bills against her palm. "Don't be silly. You can buy something for yourself, maybe have a coffee."

"I don't want to take your money."

His big hands surrounded hers, closing her fingers around the bills.

"Don't make a big deal of it, Liv. It's just a couple of bucks, and I won't have you wandering around with no money. What if something happened and you needed to get back to the house on your own?"

He was right. She was making a big deal over nothing.

She grinned. "Why? Are you planning on ditching me?"

He laughed. "I'd never do that."

She took the money and tucked it into her pocket.

He smiled. "Good. We're making some progress. Now, I'll be busy until about five, and I've made reservations at this restaurant." He handed her a card with the name Le Miroire. "As I said, it's right on the lake. It's just a few blocks from here, and you can ask anyone for directions. The people here are really friendly."

She tucked the card in her pocket with the money he'd given her. "Okay. So, are you sure you're going to a business meeting and not just grabbing a beer and playing some pool?" she asked with a grin, eyeing his biker attire.

He chuckled. "I'm sure. But maybe we can do that together after dinner." He pulled her close and gave her a kiss. Deep and delicious. When he released her, her cheeks were flushed with excitement. What she'd really like to do now was get right back on that bike and return to the house, then drag him up to the bedroom. Though thoughts of walking into a pool hall with him, all badassed and with attitude, then strolling into the back room and him taking her on a pool table flitted through her brain. Then maybe some of his friends would come in and join them, and . . .

Oh, God, what was happening to her? Her fantasies were becoming X-rated, complete with multiple big, bad biker partners.

He smiled down at her, still holding her close. "So I'll see you at five. But if you need me for any reason before that, the law firm is in this building we're in front of, so just go in and tell them and I'll be right there."

"I wouldn't interrupt your meeting," she said.

He kissed her, his lips lingering on hers. "Don't be silly. You're more important than any business meeting."

Then he released her and walked into the building. She drew in a breath, then turned and walked down the street.

* * *

"Hey, you were on Main Street about an hour ago with Shock, right?"

Liv glanced up from the bright-colored silk scarf she'd been looking at to see a lovely woman with a heart-shaped face, full lips, and big green eyes staring at her. She wore a tailored linen business suit and her long, chestnut-brown hair was neatly pinned up.

"Uh, yes."

The woman smiled and stuck out her hand. "Hi, I'm Amy. I know Shock. I work for Brenner and Brenner, the law firm he uses."

"Oh, hello." She shook the woman's hand. "He's meeting with them now, but I guess you know that if you saw us in front of the building."

"I guess you're just hanging around until his meetings are done."

"Yeah, I'm looking around, and I want to buy something for Shock."

"Oh, I could help you with that." She smiled. "You see, I know him pretty well."

At the woman's suggestive tone, Liv wondered just how well.

"I'm taking an hour break to enjoy the nice weather," Amy said. "I was just going to head over to get an ice cream. There's a place with the most amazing homemade ice cream near the park. Want to join me?"

Liv hesitated.

"Come on, I'd love the company, and we can stop by on the way to pick up something special for Shock. I guarantee, he'll love it."

"Okay."

They stopped at a little shop where there was an artisan who made mind puzzles out of wood, rope, and metal. Amy assured her that Shock loved figuring out the trick to them. Liv bought him one that consisted of two metal rods with a series of interlinked rings. Somehow, he had to extract one of the rods from the rings.

Next they walked along the tree-lined streets to a lovely little ice cream shop. They went to the counter and picked out the ice cream they wanted from the dozens of delightful flavors, then went out to the patio. Liv sat down on a decorative wrought-iron chair at a small round table, and Amy sat across from her.

Liv dipped her spoon into her pink ice cream with chocolate chunks and cherries and tasted it. Her eyes widened. "Oh, this is delicious."

"Told you so," Amy said, then enjoyed a spoonful of her orange and chocolate concoction.

"So, how long have you been dating Shock?" Amy asked.

"Oh, no, we're not dating."

"Really?" Amy's eyebrow arched. "Sorry, I saw the two of you kissing. I just assumed . . ."

Liv shrugged, feeling her cheeks heat. "It's just a casual thing."

"Hey, no need to be embarrassed." She smiled. "It was the same with us, actually." She took a bite of her ice cream. "I mean, I wanted it to be something more." She shrugged. "Who wouldn't, right? He's handsome, loaded, and . . . my God, no one is better in the sack than that man. And I mean no one."

Amy leaned in close. "So tell me," she murmured confidentially, "did he do the whole sex contract thing with you, too?"

Liv stiffened.

Amy nodded. "I see he did." She rested her arm on Liv's forearm. "Well, you're handling it the right way. Realizing it's just a casual thing. Me"—she shrugged—"I fell head over heels for him. And like a fool, I actually thought he was falling in love with me, too." She laughed. "Stupid, right?"

"He had you sign a contract, too?" Liv said numbly.

"Yeah." She patted Liv's hand and frowned. "Oh, sweetie, don't tell me you're falling for him, too?" She shook her head. "Look, I get it. He's all badass biker on the outside, yet sweet and sensitive on the inside. It's hard not to fall, and hard. But believe me, the contract means he wants to keep it on a physical level only."

She leaned in confidentially. "After it happened to me, I found out he's done it with other women, too. He uses the contract to keep a distance, I guess." She squeezed Liv's hand. "All I can say is, enjoy the ride while it lasts."

Liv walked along the street feeling numb. Shock had done this before?

She approached the restaurant and saw his motorcycle out front.

Oh, God, how would she face him knowing that she was nothing more to him than a fuck partner?

She sighed. It shouldn't matter. What they were doing was only meant to be a business relationship. He had been clear that he'd wanted her for a long time and this was a way for her to thank him. Her heart ached and she sucked in a deep breath to steady herself.

But a part of her had been hoping he would fall in love with her.

In fact, she had started to believe it was actually happening—proof that she was only seeing what she wanted to see, based on the way he treated her. The glow in his eyes when he smiled at her. His loving manner when he had sex with her. Even when he dominated her, there was a tenderness in his eyes.

Of course there was. He was a nice guy. He had always looked out for her, in his own way. He was the type of man who would make sure she got home safely from a seedy bar, and would loan her money when she needed it. Even the huge sum she'd asked for. And when he'd found out what had happened to her, and that she'd never really been with a man . . . well, of course he'd been gentle and loving with her.

But she couldn't mistake that for being in love with her.

Liv entered the restaurant and glanced around. She saw Shock sitting at a table beside the huge window overlooking the lake. As she walked toward him, her feet felt like lead.

"Hi. Did you have a good time exploring?" he asked, picking up a bottle of white wine and pouring her a glass.

"Yes, thank you," she said as she sat down. "Did your meetings go well?"

"Not as well as I'd hoped. There are still a few things I need to sort out, so I'm afraid I'll have to go back for a while after we're done here." He rested his hand on top of hers and smiled. "I promise I'll make it up to you later."

The feel of his big, warm hand on hers sent a shiver through her. Usually it would be comforting, but now she could barely stop herself from snatching her hand from his grasp.

Slowly, she drew her hand away and took a sip of her wine.

"Liv, is there something wrong?" he asked.

Her gaze lifted to his, then dropped back to the stem glass in front of her. "No, of course not."

He could probably tell it was a lie. Luckily, the waitress came by and they ordered the lasagna, which Shock told her was a specialty of the house. While they waited, Liv managed to make small talk with him, telling him about the beautiful things she'd seen in the crafts market, then giving him his gift, which he loved. But when the meal arrived, she concentrated on eating.

She debated whether to tell him she'd run into Amy, then confront him with the fact she was not the first woman he'd done this contract thing with, but her stomach knotted. What would be the point? He hadn't done anything wrong. He'd been totally aboveboard about the fact that he just wanted a physical relationship with her. What could she do? Demand he fall in love with her?

The fact that she was falling in love with him wasn't his fault. He couldn't help it that he was exactly the kind of man she'd always wanted. If things had happened differently in college—if she hadn't been scared off of having a sexual relationship with a man—then she was sure they would have become romantically involved back then. Maybe at that time she would have had a chance with him.

But clearly things had changed since then.

"Liv, what about dessert?" Shock asked.

She glanced up from her empty plate.

"What?" She'd been lost in her thoughts. She set down her fork, and the waitress, who was standing by the table, picked up her plate.

"No, thank you," Liv said.

"Just coffee," Shock said to the waitress.

But Liv didn't want to sit here over a cup of coffee with him. Watching the sun sink over the lake. Talking with him as if her heart weren't breaking.

"No coffee for me."

But the waitress had already left.

"I'm sorry, I just want to go."

"What's wrong, Liv?"

She bit her lip as she gazed into his concerned brown eyes.

"I know you have a meeting, so I'll just get a cab."

"The meeting's not important. I'll take you."

That's the last thing she wanted right now. To have her arms wrapped around him, resting her cheek against the warm, supple leather of his jacket, breathing his musky male scent as they rode back to his big house. And the bedroom they shared there.

"No . . . please. I'm not feeling well. I'd rather take a cab."

Shock turned thoughtful, but he didn't argue. He asked the waitress to arrange for a cab and soon Liv was sitting in the back of a taxi, feeling more alone than she had in years.

Liv sat in the chair by the large bedroom window watching the sun set over the lake, her knees to her chest, her arms curled around them. Shock still hadn't returned from town.

She had to get used to the idea that this month was about sex and nothing more. They even had guidelines written down so they both knew the parameters, and although at first she'd been uncomfortable with the breadth of the acts he'd included in the agreement, she'd come to see very quickly that he would never push any of them on her if they made her uncomfortable. They were simply things on the table they could try. And that meant she could trust him totally.

She had to keep a tight rein on her feelings for him.

She would concentrate on enjoying this month of physical intimacy with him. Allow it to help heal her.

There was a knock on the door and she glanced at it. Was it Raven coming to check on her again?

"Liv, it's Shock."

She drew in a breath, then dried her eyes on the hem of her T-shirt. She was surprised he'd knocked. It was his bedroom.

"May I come in?" he asked.

"Yes, of course."

The door opened and he stood there, so tall and sexy with his leather jacket unzipped, the shirt underneath stretched across his broad chest. And in his hand was the sorriest-looking bouquet of pink roses she'd ever seen.

"What's with the flowers?" she asked.

He shrugged. "I knew something was bothering you, so I wanted to bring you these to cheer you up."

He closed the door and walked toward her, holding them out.

"Watch for the thorns," he cautioned as she reached for them.

She nodded and took them from his big hand, then sniffed the poor crushed flowers.

"Sorry, I rode with them inside my jacket. It didn't work too well."

She lifted her gaze from the blossoms to his face. "It's okay. They smell lovely."

She noticed pink petals still clinging to his black T-shirt and reached for one to pluck it free. As soon as her hand touched him, he covered it with his own, pressing her fingers to his hard, muscular chest. She could feel his heart pounding.

"Liv, I'm sorry if I did something to upset you."

She shook her head. "You didn't do anything wrong."

"Then what was bothering you?"

She compressed her lips. "I guess I was just feeling a little homesick," she lied.

"Look, sweetheart, if you want to go back home, just say the word."

No, she didn't want to lose one day with him.

"I want to stay here."

He stroked her hair back. "If it's about the agreement, I'll tear it up right now. You know that."

"No, I like having this time to get to know you better." She dragged her fingertip along his lips. "And I love having sex with you."

His eyes brightened. "I like that, too."

She drew in a breath, trying to suppress the feelings rising inside her. Drowning in her need to throw herself in his arms and tell him how much she loved him.

She drew away and walked to the en suite bathroom. Shock followed on her heels. She laid the flowers at an angle in the sink, then filled it with enough water to keep them fresh until she could put them in a vase.

She loved these flowers. They were crushed and a little broken, but they still smelled sweet and looked beautiful to her. Even more so because Shock had brought them for her. He'd cradled them inside his jacket, close to his heart, to keep them safe and protected.

She could see his reflection in the mirror behind the sink, watching her, a frown on his face.

"So you're totally comfortable with the agreement? Even when I command you to do things? Or restrain your hands so you can't escape?"

Her breath caught. "Actually, I find that very exciting."

"And what about some of those things that made you uncomfortable?" He moved closer.

"What if I turned you around and leaned you forward?" He did just that, pressing her forward and leaning her over the vanity. He glided his hand over her ass and cupped. "And pushed into you here?"

He pressed his fingers against the middle seam of her jeans, leaving no doubt he was talking about anal sex.

Her inside muscles tightened and anxiety rippled through her, but she calmed herself.

"It would be fine. I've never done it before, but I trust you to guide me through it."

His reflected gaze locked on hers and his pupils dilated, making his brown eyes go almost black. "You trust me."

"Of course."

He pulled her against his chest, his arms wrapping around her waist, and held her. The deeply serious look on his face as he stared at her reflection stirred something deep inside her.

"I want you to trust me. I want you to know I'll never hurt you."

She nodded. "I do know that."

He turned her to face him and swept her into his arms, then their lips met and she got lost in the sweep of emotions that emanated from him to her, sending her senses reeling.

Their mouths parted and his lips brushed against her temple.

"I want you to promise if I push something too fast or too far . . . if I do anything to make you uncomfortable . . . you'll let me know."

"I will. I promise."

She smiled and gazed down at the flowers lying in the sink. "I love the roses. Thank you so much."

He tightened his arms around her and she kissed him again, melting into his embrace.

She curled her arms around his neck, staring up at him. "I can't believe you remembered I like pink roses."

He took her hand and led her back into the bedroom.

"How could I forget how much you gushed when your sister sent you some on your twenty-second birthday?"

She laughed and stroked his chest. "So I have a question. Would it break the terms of the agreement if I were to kiss you, then initiate sex?"

He smiled and ran his hands up her sides, his thumbs tracing the curves of her breasts, making her long for him to cover them with his big, warm palms. Her nipples hardened at the thought.

"Not at all. I would love it," he murmured against her ear, sending tingles down her spine.

She leaned in and nuzzled his neck, loving the roughness of his coarse stubble against her lips. "I'm glad," she whispered, sliding her hand down his chest, then over his thickening bulge under the denim.

She unzipped them and put her hand inside.

Shock's breath caught as her soft fingers wrapped around him. God, there'd been so much turmoil between them. All he wanted to do was to make love to her. Sweetly and tenderly.

He captured her lips again as she stroked him, a wave of pleasure surging through him.

"Oh, baby, what you're doing feels so good." He held her tighter, enjoying everything about her body against his, her gentle touch arousing him.

He wanted to touch her, too. To taste her and bring her to orgasm while she called out his name.

Someone rapped loudly on the door and he ignored it. He caressed her breast, anticipating taking the sweet bud in his mouth.

"Shock." It was Rip's voice.

Shock dragged his mouth from Liv's. "What?" he barked.

"There's a call for you."

"Take a fucking message."

"Man, it's from a hospital. Something about Liv's sister."

Liv's eyes went wide and her hand slipped away from him. Shock zipped up as he strode to the door, Liv on his heels. As soon as he pulled it open, Rip held out the phone. Liv took it.

"Hello? This is Olivia Hughes. You're calling about my sister, Julia?"

Shock watched her as she listened, his gut clenching as tears glistened in her eyes.

"I understand. Yes. I . . ." Her voice broke and Shock's stomach twisted. He placed his hand on her shoulder and squeezed gently.

She sucked in a breath. "Yes, thank you." Her voice was soft. Resigned.

She handed the phone back to Rip.

"Julia . . . my sister. She's in the hospital."

Shock nodded, waiting for her to tell him what she had to say in her own time.

"She's been really sick and . . . they said she's taken a turn for the worse."

Her hand clamped on Shock's forearm and her fingers

dug into him. "They said . . ." She sucked in a ragged breath and couldn't continue.

"What is it, Liv?" he prompted. "Tell me."

She gazed up at him, her eyes blue pools of pain. "They said she's dying."

Part Three

Shock watched helplessly as Liv's eyes flooded with tears. He pulled her into his arms and held her, but she was stiff and unresponsive.

"We'll go see her right now," he said.

"But . . ." She choked back a sob. "We're so far away."

It was true the drive here had taken the better part of a day.

"I know, but I'll get you there in three hours. Rip, stay with her while I make some calls."

As Liv watched Shock stride from the room, she felt guilty for having been so stiff in his arms, but she couldn't give herself over to the comfort he offered. She couldn't allow herself to start relying on him, even for emotional support.

A few minutes later, Steele and Tempest came to the door.

"What's going on?" Steele asked.

"Liv's sister is"—Rip glanced at Liv uncomfortably—"in the hospital."

"She's dying," Liv said. Oh, God, how could this be happening? She'd done everything she could to prevent this. To see that her sister got healthy again.

She wobbled as her knees threatened to buckle, and Rip caught her elbow, then led her to the bed. She sank onto it. Tempest hurried over and sat down beside her. Liv welcomed the feel of the other woman's arm around her waist. She rested her head on Tempest's shoulder, needing the warmth and comfort of another person desperately.

A moment later, someone handed her a glass of water and she took a sip, still trying to stifle her sobs.

"Do you want to talk about it?" Tempest asked, her lovely face filled with warmth and concern.

Liv drew in a deep breath. Maybe it would help.

"Julia's been sick for quite a while now. She's been in the hospital. I thought—" Her throat closed up and her fingers clenched into a fist as pain tore through her. She sucked in a breath as a tear streamed down her cheek.

Tempest pulled her close and hugged her and Liv settled into the hug, resting her head on Tempest's shoulder and closing her eyes. Tempest stroked her back and Liv soaked in the warmth and support.

When she had collected herself, Liv sat up, wiping her eyes. "I thought she was getting better. They did surgery and they thought she was improving. I . . ." She pushed away the insistent tears. "I never would have left her otherwise. Now she's unconscious and unresponsive."

Tempest squeezed her arm and handed her the glass of water again. She sipped, but her hand was unsteady, so Steele took it from her and Tempest pulled her into a hug again. Steele put his hand on her back, and Liv felt grateful for their presence.

"Oh, Liv, I'm so sorry," Tempest said.

Liv just nodded.

"Liv."

Liv eased away from Tempest, her gaze locking on Shock, who stood in the doorway.

"I've arranged a flight. A car will be here in five minutes."

Liv stood up, feeling shaky. "I need to pack."

"Don't worry about it. We'll buy what we need when we get there."

"I want my bag," she said adamantly as she stood up. She walked to the closet where she'd stowed it and pulled it out, then walked into the bathroom and started tossing things into it, like her hair dryer, toothpaste, and moisturizer. She didn't know why, but she had to have her bag. She had to have her things, even if it was just a collection of toiletries, like her own hairbrush.

Shock followed her into the room and rested his hands on her shoulders.

"Liv, it's okay. You really don't need to worry about this right now."

"I . . ." Then her chin quivered and tears fell from her eyes. "I just . . . I'll feel better with my own stuff."

He squeezed her shoulders gently. "Whatever you want, sweetheart."

He helped her pack the things into her backpack. Once the counter was clear, she glanced around helplessly.

"Liv," Shock said softly, "why don't we go now?"

Why? Maybe if she stayed here—if she ignored the call from the hospital altogether—she could make herself believe it wasn't true. That Julia wasn't really . . .

Tears welled in her eyes again and rolled down her cheeks. A sob clutched her throat and escaped.

"Oh, God, Liv."

Shock swept her into his arms and this time she welcomed him. Her arms wrapped around his big solid body and she let him pull her tight to him, then melted against him.

"Shock, I . . ." Her tears flowed freely now.

Shock's lips brushed the top of her head in a kiss. "What is it, sweetheart?"

"I don't want my sister to die."

"I know, sweetheart. Neither do I. And we'll do everything we can to stop that from happening."

Shock took Liv's hand and helped her from the town car. A driver had picked them up from the house and got them to the airport in twenty minutes. Now the private jet he'd arranged was waiting for them.

Liv sank into the cream-colored leather seat and Shock sat across from her. Soon they were in the air.

Shock watched her. In the hustle of getting here, they hadn't really spoken. He hadn't wanted to push her to talk.

"Liv, that's why you needed the money? To help your sister?"

She bit her lip and nodded.

"Why didn't you tell me your sister was sick and that's what the money was for?"

She looked blankly at her hands folded in her lap, and her eyes were wet. "I don't know. I guess I . . . didn't want to beg for my sister's life."

"Ah, Liv."

Then she shook her head, her fingers gripping the armrests of her seat. "I also didn't want you to pity me. I've always valued your opinion of me and I guess that didn't change even after we lost touch. And if I'm being completely honest I think . . . I guess I wanted to know if you'd actually lend it to me . . . just because I asked. I didn't want to have to prove that what I needed it for was worthy."

"You wanted to know if I trusted you."

She nodded. "At least, that you trusted my judgment."

He leaned back in his seat. "You know, I actually thought you were borrowing it for that guy I saw you with. You never denied it."

She pursed her lips. "But you lent it to me anyway."

"Of course I did. And now I know what it was really for." He reached out and took her hand, then enveloped it in his own. "Liv, I'm so sorry about your sister."

She just nodded and held his hand tighter. "You know, I just can't believe I might lose her."

She looked so fragile sitting there, her eyes shimmering.

She drew a deep breath. "I still remember when I was about four years old and Mom got Julia a teddy bear. It was brown with a plaid bow around its neck and she called it Mac." She smiled tremulously. "And it was so soft and cuddly. I picked it up and hugged it and I fell in love with it. I didn't want to let it go. Julia and I shared a room and she let me sleep with it that first night. In the morning, I didn't want to give it up. Instead of being upset, when she saw how much I loved it, she told Mom that she wanted me to have it." She stared at her hands, her lip quivering. "Even at eight years old, she took care of me. And as we grew up, she always looked out for me like that. That's why"—her eyes met his—"I'll do anything I can to save her."

He leaned in and held her close. "I know, sweetheart. And I'll help you in any way I can."

Liv wasn't prepared for the sight of her sister, hooked up to monitors and machines, her face so pale she looked like a ghost. Liv hurried to the bed and rested her hand on Julia's.

"She's in an induced coma, so she won't regain consciousness," the nurse said to Shock, who'd followed her in, "but you're both welcome to sit with her as long as you like."

A moment later, she felt Shock at her side.

"Liv, sit." He had pulled a chair close to the bed. Liv sank into it.

He pulled over another chair and sat beside her. He rested his hand on her arm as she sat staring at Julia, pain gnawing at her insides. She barely noticed Shock beside her, but on some level, his warmth and strength helped.

Time passed, she didn't know how much. Shock went to talk to the nurse for a little while, but other than that, he stayed by her side. He offered to get her a coffee a couple of times, which she declined.

The hospital was quiet. They'd arrived after midnight

and she knew it was the wee hours, but slowly light crept into the room with the rising sun.

She could sense the increased activity around them, which made her feel even more weary than she was. The nurse who had led them into Julia's room had stopped by several times during the night, but now a new nurse showed up to check Julia's chart.

Shock excused himself, then returned a few minutes later.

"I talked to the nurse and she said the doctor will want to talk to you, but he won't be available until this afternoon. Why don't we go get a few hours' sleep?"

Liv was exhausted and knew what he suggested was wise. She nodded and squeezed Julia's hand, then let Shock lead her out the door.

"Liv. It's time to wake up."

Liv opened her eyes and glanced around, disoriented. She was lying in a soft, cozy bed, sunlight streaming in the window.

She blinked as she glanced up at Shock, who stood leaning over her.

"Where am I?"

"You're in the hotel."

She sat up. "How's Julia? Can I go see her now?"

Fear jolted through her. What if she'd slept too long? What if Julia was . . . if she . . .

"Yes, that's why I called you. The doctor wants to speak with you. Then you can see Julia."

Liv stood up and hurried to the bathroom to wash her

face, then she followed Shock from the room. After a short cab ride, they stepped off the elevator and went to the nurses' station near Julia's room.

Shock spoke with the woman behind the counter, then someone led them to an office. She and Shock sat in the two guest chairs facing a small desk and waited.

A tall, blond doctor stepped into the room and closed the door behind him. "Hello, I'm Dr. Greyson," he said. "Miss Hughes?"

"Yes." Liv watched him sit in the chair behind the desk, her stomach clenching, afraid of what he might be about to tell them.

"As you know, we thought your sister was in remission after the surgery, but then she took a downward turn. We put her into a medically induced coma until we could talk to you and decide what course of action to take."

Liv nodded. "They called yesterday and told me that . . ." She bit her lip, trying to stop it from quivering. "That she was dying."

"Well, we didn't have many options, and most of them were very expensive and with no guarantees." His kind blue eyes locked on her. "Now, however, I have some promising news. It seems that there might be another course of action we can take. We did some tests earlier today—they were on the recommendation of a specialist from another hospital who has had great success in these cases—and it looks like there is a very new, very experimental drug we could try."

"Really?" Hope rose in her.

"And don't worry about the cost and the insurance

stuff—I'll handle all that," Shock said, squeezing her shoulder.

Anxiety washed through her. "I can't let you—"

"Nonsense," Shock said, cutting her off.

"We can start right away and we'll know if it's successful in a few days." Dr. Greyson placed some paperwork and a pen in front of her. "All I need is for you to sign the forms."

Shock picked up the pen and handed it to her. She took it and signed the forms, then handed them back to the doctor.

"Good. We'll get started right away."

That night, as soon as Shock turned out the light, Liv rested her head against his chest and listened to the steady rhythm of his heart.

"I want to thank you for being here for me," she said in the darkness.

He stroked her hair. "Where else would I be?"

"You could have gone back with your friends and just waited for me."

He tightened his arms around her.

"No. I really couldn't have done that." He kissed the top of her head. "Now get some sleep."

She used to get annoyed when he told her what to do, but now she knew it was because he cared about her, not because he was trying to control her. Or that he thought she couldn't take care of herself. He was just . . . being supportive. And right now, she really needed that.

.   .   .

The next few days were one big blur. Julia wasn't awake very often, and when she was, she wasn't very coherent, but by the third day the doctor called them into his office again and told them that the treatment had worked and Julia was going to be fine.

"Hey, you're looking pretty good," Liv said as she and Shock walked into Julia's room.

Julia was sitting in one of the armchairs.

"I'm feeling pretty good. I went for a walk up and down the hall. Now I'm having a rest. This afternoon I'm going out to the courtyard to enjoy the sunshine."

Liv sat on the side of the bed, and Shock sat in the guest chair.

"That's great. That'll be good for you." She took Julia's hand and smiled. "I was so afraid I was going to lose you. I can't tell you how happy I am that you're going to be all right."

Julia squeezed her hand. "I know, Livvy. And I appreciate all you've done for me. I really do."

Julia glanced at Shock. "So who's this?"

"I'm Devin," Shock said with a charming smile. "Liv and I knew each other in college."

"Oh, that's nice," Julia said with a big smile.

Liv was relieved that Julia didn't say anything about how she used to gush about Devin.

Shock stood up. "I know the two of you have a lot to talk about so I'll leave you alone."

Liv watched him leave, then turned to Julia again. Julia looked at her with a smug smile.

"So tell me about this guy. He's pretty sexy. And he

doesn't look anything like what I expected from your description of him in college. I would have expected someone in an expensive suit, not jeans and tattoos."

"He's changed since college. Left the family business and made his own fortune. Now he spends his time traveling with his friends."

She squeezed Liv's hand. "So, is it serious between you?"

"What?" She glanced down at her hand. "No, not really."

"Are you sure? Because when he looks at you . . ."

Liv was surprised. "When he looks at me what?"

Julia shrugged. "I think he's really hung up on you."

Liv's stomach clenched. "Let's change the subject. Did they tell you when you're getting out of the hospital?"

"In about a week." She took Liv's hand. "I'll still need intensive outpatient therapy, but it'll be nice to be home. My friend Jenn is going to come stay with me for a while. You remember her?"

Liv had met Jenn a couple of times. She was actually a nurse, so Julia would be in good hands.

"That's great. I just want to let you know I'm going to be out of town for a few weeks."

"With Devin?" Julia asked, with a devilish grin.

Liv wanted to deny it, but she couldn't lie to her sister, so she nodded.

"Good. You do that. And you don't need to worry about me. I want you to concentrate on that sexy man of yours."

·   ·   ·

When Liv got back to Shock's country house, the others were very solicitous about her sister. Shock had kept them updated about her sister's recovery, so they knew the basics, but they all made Liv feel very special and cared for.

She might not be used to having friends, but she understood that her relationship with Julia had helped her to accept comfort from Tempest and Raven. But she was surprised at how she was also comfortable with the men's attention. Usually, she found it difficult to accept the attention of men, always being a little fearful they just wanted something from her. But these men—Shock's friends— actually made her feel that they really cared about her and what she was going through.

It was a strange feeling.

Finally, Shock took her hand and explained to them all that she was tired from the trip, then led her upstairs. As soon as the door closed on their bedroom, she slipped into his embrace and hugged him. His arms came around her and they stayed like that for several long moments, Liv just soaking in the loving, protective feel of his body enveloping her.

When they parted, she walked to the love seat by the window and sat down. He sat down beside her.

"We haven't talked about this," she said. "I haven't wanted to talk about this . . ."

Shock took her hand. The feel of his big fingers enveloping hers filled her with warmth.

"You're responsible for my sister's recovery," she continued, "and I really want to thank you."

"I was happy to help," he said gently.

"It must have been expensive." Her stomach knotted at the thought.

"Don't worry about it."

"But I need to pay you back."

"No you don't. I couldn't just watch while someone you cared about died. I didn't do it expecting you or anyone else to pay me back." He stroked her hair from her face. "You know, you don't have to take on the responsibilities of the world."

Her throat tightened. She'd always thought he believed she was irresponsible and flighty, so those words meant the world to her.

She rested her hand on his arm. "You saved my sister's life. I don't know how to thank you for that."

He drew her close. "I would have done anything to help."

Her heart ached. "How do I ever repay you?"

"You don't."

She just gazed at him. How had she been so lucky to have found Shock again?

Her heart clenched. If only it could be more than just a month.

She reached out and stroked his cheek. "Thank you for being here for me. And for helping me so much."

Shock couldn't drag his gaze from hers. The feel of her soft hand on his cheek sent need rushing through him. He wanted to protect this woman. To fold her into his arms and hold her close, keeping everything bad in the world at bay.

He'd stayed by her side at the hospital and done everything he could to help her through her ordeal. And he'd put no demands on her. But as she stroked his cheek now, his body tightened and his longing for her became almost overwhelming.

She tipped up her face, her full lips a temptation he could barely resist. But he didn't have to because she leaned closer and kissed him.

He tightened his arms around her, pulling her close.

Her lips moved on his, her arms sliding around his neck, then her tongue pressed into his mouth and he nearly groaned. The velvety feel of it gliding against his own sent his heartbeat racing. He loved the sweet taste of her and the feel of her soft body against him.

Then she drew back and stared at him with wide eyes.

"Oh, God, I want you, Shock. Please make love to me."

His heart pounded at the need in her voice and heat rushed through him.

"I want you, too, baby."

He captured her lips, plunging his tongue inside her mouth. She sucked on it and he groaned.

It had been too long since he'd been with her like this, and he was overwhelmed by his incredible desire for her.

But he'd go slowly.

Her delicate lips nuzzled against his neck and she glided her hand down his chest. When her hand reached the growing bulge in his pants, he sucked in a breath.

Her fingers wrapped around him and she squeezed.

He couldn't stand it anymore. He had to feel flesh on flesh. He stood up and stripped off his jeans, then tugged his T-shirt over his head. As she watched him with wide eyes, he pushed down his boxers, then kicked them away. She stroked his stomach, then wrapped her hand around him again.

She locked gazes with him as she leaned in and nuzzled the tip of his cock with her lips. Then she opened and swallowed his shaft.

"Oh, God, Liv, that feels so good." He rested his hand on her head and tangled his fingers in her long, silky hair.

She glided forward, still gazing at him with heated blue eyes. As she took him deeper, her fingertips slid under his balls, and she cupped them in her hand.

She drew back and glided forward again, taking him impossibly deep.

His insides quivered at the sensations blasting through him. He had to stop himself from thrusting forward into her mouth. He guided her head lightly as she moved back and forth. He wanted her so badly. His cock ached with the need to release.

It wouldn't take long before he would erupt in her mouth. But that wasn't what he wanted. Right now he wanted her cradled against his body, naked and trembling in his arms, as he drove into her warm, welcoming body.

"Liv, stop," he said, as he gently guided her head back.

His cock slipped from her mouth, but she still held it in her delicate hands.

"I want to see you. To make love to you," he explained.

She nodded and stood up, then pulled off her shirt. He

watched in anticipation as she unfastened her bra and drew it from her body, then let it drop to the floor.

His gaze settled on her round, full breasts, the nipples swollen with need. He brushed one with his fingers as she unfastened her jeans. She pushed them down, along with her panties, then stepped out of them.

Now she stood before him naked and the sight took his breath away. She was so perfect in every way.

Shock cupped her breasts, feeling the weight of them in his hands, lifting them gently. Then he leaned forward and tasted one sweet nipple. It hardened in his mouth, the areola pebbling as he drew it inside. He ran his tongue over it, then suckled, delighting in her soft moan.

He swept her up in his arms and carried her to the big, king-size bed and laid her down gently in the center. Then he knelt on the bed, between her knees and pressed her legs wide. He gazed at her bare pussy and smiled.

"You are so beautiful." He stroked it, loving the feel of her soft skin beneath his fingertips.

He opened the folds, gazing at her glistening opening.

"You're ready for me, aren't you, sweetheart?"

"So ready," she said with longing in her eyes.

His heart swelled. She wanted him.

He stroked her slick inner folds, the feel of her desire sending him careening off balance. His pulse pounded in his ears as he leaned forward, breathing in the musky feminine scent of her. Then he lapped his tongue over her damp flesh and she moaned, arching beneath him. He dragged his thumbs along her folds, then drew them apart to reveal her clit.

What a beautiful sight. The key to her pleasure.

He pressed his tongue to her damp flesh, then circled the little bud. Round and round with the tip of his tongue.

She moaned, tossing her head back and forth on the pillow.

He could bring her to orgasm like this quickly. He knew that. All he had to do was suckle her sweet button, and maybe glide his fingers in and out of her clenching passage.

And he should. He should give her that pleasure.

But right now he wanted to be inside her. He wanted them to find their pleasure together.

He lifted his head and gazed at her, his thumb lightly teasing her clit. She whimpered softly.

"Baby, I'm going to make love to you now."

"Yes," she murmured, and opened her arms to him.

He smiled, his heart swelling at her tender welcome. He wrapped his hand around his cock, aching to be inside her, and pressed the tip to her slick opening.

He pressed forward a little, mesmerized by the warmth of her against him. As he moved, oh, so slowly, he delighted in the feel of her opening around him. A little more and his cockhead was fully immersed and gliding deeper into her yielding flesh.

Her eyes closed and she murmured softly.

He moved slowly, savoring every inch.

"Oh, yes," she murmured. "You feel so good inside me."

Her words shimmered through him, driving his need

higher. He pushed the last inch into her, now fully inside her hot, welcoming channel.

He stayed like that, his body pressed tightly to hers, his cock throbbing inside her.

She opened her eyes and they were filled with longing. "Please, Shock. I need you."

He drew back, his cock squeezed tight by her intimate flesh, then glided forward again. She grasped his shoulders, her eyes wide and locked on his.

"Do you like that, sweetheart?" he asked.

He drew back and plunged deep again.

"Ohhhh, yes."

The sound of her desire drove him wild. As her murmurs of pleasure increased, he thrust faster. Filling her deeper. Harder.

She clutched his shoulders more tightly. "Shock . . . I'm so close."

Fuck, he was, too. But he'd wait for her pleasure first.

He drove into her, again and again, his groin tightening as he held back his release.

Then she threw her head back and moaned. He watched in awe as he thrust into her, pleasure shining in her eyes, glowing from her like a golden sun. She gasped, then wailed. Long and loud. He pumped into her, driving her pleasure on and on.

Then his own pleasure swelled and burst, surging through him like hot lava erupting from the earth's core. He shuddered at the intensity of it, holding her warm body tightly to him, her soft moans echoing in his ears.

Still floating on a cloud of delight, he slumped on the

bed, then rolled back, keeping her body snug against his, both of them still breathing heavily. He kissed the top of her head as he held it to his chest, close to his heart, then stroked her hair.

He couldn't believe how much he wanted to be with this woman. He'd never wanted anyone more. And that meant he had to make some decisions. Tomorrow, he'd go into town and set things in motion.

Liv woke up in Shock's arms, snuggled against his chest. She opened her eyes and breathed in his musky male scent, loving the feel of being cocooned in his embrace.

She felt so close to him.

Last night had been special. His lovemaking had been poignant and tender, and the look in his eyes had been loving. Maybe he'd started this whole thing because he wanted to enjoy a short-term physical relationship with her, but was it possible that he was actually falling in love with her?

She nuzzled his chest.

Shock kissed the top of her head. "Hey, sleepyhead. You ready to get up?"

"Mmm. I guess so." She tilted her face up and smiled.

He leaned down and captured her lips in a sweet, loving kiss. Then he rolled to a sitting position and stood up. "How about we do breakfast, then go for a walk? There's a nice path around the lake. Or we could just go out in the canoe."

She and Shock used to go for walks sometimes when they were back in college. Usually after they'd spent a while poring over homework and needed a break. He'd always seemed to know when she'd had enough. Even though she would keep pushing through, he'd suggest they take a breather, insisting the break would revive them. And he was always right. Afterward, solutions that had been stumping her seemed to pop right into her brain.

If they had gotten involved back then, it would have been like this. Waking up in each other's arms, going for walks. Making love whenever they wanted.

She sighed and got out of bed. "A walk sounds nice."

It was warm and sunny out and they enjoyed the morning. Walking by the lake, a light breeze rustling through the trees. The loons calling over the water.

They walked hand in hand and she felt safe and protected with him. She wanted to feel like this always.

After lunch, Shock told her he had to go into town to finish up some business and asked her to join him. Once they got into town, he dropped her off near the crafts market, where she wandered around admiring the handiwork in the delightful shops.

When she tired of that, she decided to go to the same little ice cream parlor where she'd gone with Amy.

The young woman behind the counter smiled. "Back again?"

She was the same woman who had served her and Amy last time. Her name tag said her name was Jan.

"That's right. I want to try one of those," Liv said, pointing at the orange and chocolate swirl ice cream Amy had had last time. "It looks so good."

She took the bowl the woman handed her and carried

it to one of the tables by the window, then enjoyed the view as she ate.

She glanced up as the bell over the door rang. Amy walked into the shop and glanced toward her. She smiled and waved at Liv, but didn't seem surprised to see her. She exchanged some words with Jan, then a few minutes later walked toward Liv's table with a bowl of ice cream in her hand.

"Mind if I join you?" she asked.

"No. Please do."

Amy set her bowl on the table and sat down. "So, how are things going?"

Liv shrugged. "Fine."

She wasn't really sure what to say to this woman, who had been one of Shock's previous lovers. Especially now that Liv thought maybe there was a chance for Shock and her to be together. After last night . . .

"You look different," Amy said. "Happier." Her lips pursed. "Does this mean you're falling for the guy?"

Liv pushed the tip of her spoon into the ice cream, then toyed with it. She didn't really know what to say.

"Look, I know you don't know me," Amy said. "And there's no reason for you to talk to me. But I've been thinking about you. I remember how painful it was for me when he broke it off, and how much of a fool I felt when I realized that there had never been a chance for us." She placed her hand on Liv's. "I know how easy it is to fall in love with him. And I see it in your eyes. You have fallen for him, haven't you?"

"Amy, I appreciate that you want to help, but what

you don't know is that I've known Shock for a long time. We went to college together and"—Liv adjusted the cloth napkin on her lap—"I believe he does have feelings for me."

Amy stared at her, her mouth pinched in anxiety. "Oh, no, honey. Don't fool yourself."

Liv frowned. "I don't know why you think you know him better than I do."

Amy leaned forward, her face serious. "Because I do."

The woman was making Liv nervous. The tension and intensity emanating from her were quite different from the easygoing attitude she'd had last time.

"The man has secrets," Amy said. "Believe me, there's a lot you don't know about him. Things he'll never tell you." She rested her hand on the table. It was clenched into a fist. "Things that will shatter this cozy little dream you're wrapping yourself in."

Liv's stomach clenched. "You make it sound like he's some kind of criminal or something."

Was that it? Did Amy know about Shock's father and brother embezzling from the family business? Did she think Shock had been a part of that? He'd told Liv he hadn't been, and he hadn't had to tell her about it at all. But could he have been involved?

Even if he had been, would Liv feel any differently about him? With everything he'd done for her, she knew she wouldn't. Even if he had been involved, which she really didn't believe, he was a changed person now.

She put down her spoon and locked gazes with the woman. "What are these secrets?"

Amy glanced around nervously. "I could lose my job if I tell you."

Anger flowed through Liv. "Look, you're the one who came to me and claimed he has all these secrets. So tell me, what secrets does Shock have that will make a difference to me?"

Amy leaned in closer. "Well, for starters, did he tell you he's married?"

Liv felt as if the ground had dropped out from under her, and she could only stare at Amy in disbelief.

"I don't expect you to believe me," Amy said, pulling out her phone and scrolling through it. "But I'm sure you'll believe your own eyes."

A moment later, Amy handed Liv her phone, which displayed a picture of Shock in a tuxedo, his arm wrapped possessively around a beautiful bride, and his wedding ring impossible to miss.

A half hour later, Liv watched as Shock roared down Main Street on his bike and stopped at the corner where he'd said he'd pick her up. Stiffly, she walked toward him, trying to hide the raw emotions tearing her apart inside. She tried to paste on a fake smile and failed miserably, but he didn't seem to notice as he turned to grab her helmet, then handed it to her.

"Have a good time?" he asked as she mounted the bike.

"Yes," she said, as she pulled on the helmet.

She wrapped her arms around his waist, her hands resting on his hard, flat stomach as the engine roared and he took off down the street.

As they passed the law firm, she saw Amy sitting on the steps, smoking a cigarette with some other women. Amy watched her as they passed by, looking somber.

Sadness gripped her and she rested her head against Shock's back. The supple leather was soft against her cheek and she breathed in the musky scent of it.

Any hope she'd had of having a real relationship with Shock had been dashed by those two words Amy had uttered. *He's married.*

She wanted to be mad. To hate him for leading her on.

But he wasn't. He'd never said he wanted anything more than one month of physical intimacy with her. He'd even laid out a contract.

Amy had explained that Shock's wife knew about these little affairs he had and was okay with it, especially if he did the contracts. That way the women knew it was only a short-term thing. As far as Liv was concerned, that was pretty fucked up—it certainly wasn't the way she would want a relationship to be—but it wasn't her relationship, and it wasn't up to her to judge.

As much as she wanted to be angry with him, really she just felt sad. And sorry for herself.

But she reminded herself that Shock was also being a good friend to her. He was helping her, both financially and emotionally. He was being caring and supportive in helping her get over her sexual issues.

In fact, she felt a little sad for him because he didn't have a wife who loved him enough to ride with him and keep him happy all the time.

Which she would. If she were lucky enough to have Shock as her man, she would never leave his side.

．　　．　　．

When they arrived at the house, the men started a barbecue and put on some steaks. Liv and Raven made a salad and Tempest prepared a pitcher of sangria. Soon they were sitting around the large picnic table in the yard, eating and laughing.

Liv finished her glass of sangria and Magic filled it up again. She was feeling a little more relaxed, and when Shock slid his arm around her, she leaned against him, deciding to put aside her sadness and just enjoy the time she still had with him.

When Shock had proposed their little arrangement, she never would have guessed that it would turn out this way. That she'd fall for him . . . and that he was already attached. But if she was truly honest with herself, she didn't regret anything that had happened with Shock.

He'd helped her save her sister's life. He'd been there for her when she needed him most. And he'd even helped her confront what had happened to her in college, showing her how to enjoy being with a man.

Now she chose to focus on the positive rather than allowing the whole experience to leave her broken and bitter.

She noticed Rip had his arm around Raven, who was whispering in his ear and smiling.

"Well, if you're hot, I have a solution to that," Rip said. Then he scooped her up and carried her across the lawn to the pool.

"Don't you dare," she squealed as she clung to his neck.

"What was that, woman?" He grinned. "A dare?"

Then he tossed her into the pool. She shrieked as she hit the water with a big splash. Tempest raced up behind Rip and pushed him, but he grabbed her and they both fell into the water.

Laughing and yelling, the three of them climbed out of the pool.

"You got my favorite jeans wet," Raven complained, then unfastened them and pushed them down.

Liv watched wide-eyed as both women stripped off their clothes and tossed them on the grass, thankfully stopping at their underwear. Raven wore a black bra, edged with red satin ribbon, that plunged so low, Liv feared her large breasts would tumble out. Tempest wore a royal blue lace bra that lifted and displayed her perfectly formed breasts quite nicely. Both women wore thongs that matched their bras. It was like they wore elegant bikinis, but way sexier because these lovely undergarments were not meant to be seen in public.

Rip stripped off his wet T-shirt and dropped his jeans to the ground, then he pulled Raven against him and kissed her. Long and passionately.

"Mmm, sweetie," Raven murmured when he released her lips. "I think you need some cooling off."

Raven started pushing him toward the water, but he just laughed and scooped her up, the bulge in his boxers evident, then raced toward the pool again. He leaped into the deep end with her in his arms.

Tempest glanced at Steele with her expressive blue eyes while his heated gaze glided over her body. "Coming?" she asked.

"Oh, very nearly," he said, then stood up.

Liv watched as Steele stripped off his shirt, revealing his bulging muscles and the snake tattoo coiling around his bicep, then across his chest. Then he pushed down his jeans. The other men took off their clothes, too, except Shock who still sat by her side. Her pulse quickened at the sight of their big, muscular, inked bodies.

Shock's lips brushed against her ear. "You want to go for a swim, too?"

Liv's insides quivered. She wanted to. She wished she was bold enough to stand up and strip down in front of these men. To bask in the warmth of their desire. Then to open her arms to them in blatant invitation.

She bit her lip and gazed at him. Was this what he wanted? Did he intend to share her with the other men right now? Her insides quivered with both nervousness and excitement.

"I . . . uh . . . I'm not sure . . ." she said nervously.

"It's okay, sweetheart. I just mean a swim."

She gazed into his reassuring brown eyes and he drew her close and kissed her.

When he released her lips, she nodded, knowing Shock wouldn't push her to do more than she wanted to.

She glanced at Tempest and Raven, who were sitting on the edge of the pool in their bras and panties, dangling their legs in the water, totally unembarrassed by the fact their thongs covered nothing of their derrieres at all, and their sexy, low-cut bras showed off the swell of their round, full breasts to anyone who cared to look. And the men, who were all now in the pool, were looking.

She wanted to learn to be more comfortable with her sexuality, and this was a perfect opportunity. Swimming in front of a bunch of sexy men in her underwear seemed a pretty modest start. It wasn't like they were all naked. At least, not yet.

She stood up and pulled her T-shirt over her head. She was a little embarrassed when she realized Wild Card's warm hazel eyes were focused on her, but she pushed it aside, reminding herself that Wild Card had already seen her totally topless anyway.

She removed her jeans and stood up, wearing only her baby-blue bra and matching panties. At least hers covered her ass so she didn't feel quite so conspicuous.

Shock stripped off his clothes, too, then watched her as she walked to the side of the pool and dove in, then glided through the water. She surfaced and shook her head, flinging water droplets around her, then swam to the shallow end where Wild Card sat on the wide steps and Magic and Dom stood in the water.

God, these men were so good-looking. Magic with his James Dean–style hair and magical smile. Dom, taller than the other two, with his short-cropped hair and a fringe of whiskers along his chin. And Wild Card, with his dark blond spiked hair and warm, disarming smile. They were all broad-shouldered, muscular, and adorned with tattoos. So sexy.

As soon as her feet felt the bottom of the pool, she stood up and walked toward Shock. He took her hand and led her to the steps, then sat down beside Wild Card and opened his arms to her. She sat on the step in front of him, facing the water, and he wrapped his arms around her.

Across the pool, Rip and Raven were kissing and Liv realized he was unfastening her bra. It released and Raven stripped it off and allowed it to float away. He began kissing her breasts. Her head dropped back and the sunlight glistened on her black, glossy hair.

Liv drew in a deep breath, imagining herself walking toward Wild Card, reaching around behind herself and unfastening her bra. She would lock gazes with him as she dropped the bra straps from her shoulders and slid them off, then peeled the bra from her wet breasts.

His heated gaze would drop to her naked mounds, the nipples hard from the cool water. Then he'd cup one of her breasts and lift, the feel of his big hand around her soft flesh sending heat coursing through her.

He would ease his face forward and—

"Sweetheart, are you sure you're okay staying here?" Shock asked.

She glanced around and realized Rip was driving into Raven, to her ecstatic moans. Dom and Magic were sitting side by side in front of Tempest as she stroked Dom's cock and sucked on Magic. Steele stood behind her, cupping her breasts in his big hands. Liv suspected that his big cock was pressed between her thighs, rubbing against her intimate flesh.

Oh, God, she wanted to join them. To have three men paying total attention to her. She wanted to feel their cocks in her hand. In her mouth. To feel their big hands on her. To feel a hot mouth on each of her breasts.

She locked gazes with Shock and said with confidence, "Yes, I'm sure." Then she cupped his raspy face and leaned forward, brushing her lips against his.

Butterflies fluttered through her stomach, but she quelled her nervousness as she buoyed her courage to tell him she wanted to be with the other men.

His hand brushed over her breast and he stroked it as he rested his cheek against hers.

"Are you getting turned on?"

Her nipple was a hard, aching bud pushing against his palm through the lace.

"Yes," she murmured.

His hand slid down her waist, then over the crotch of her panties. She felt a little embarrassed, but no one was looking their way. They were all busy with their own passionate actions.

His finger dipped under her panties and stroked her hot folds.

"Fuck, you are really wet."

His arm tightened around her and he tipped up her face with his free hand and kissed her passionately. When he eased away, his hot gaze locked on hers.

"I think we should go upstairs."

"But . . ."

He nuzzled her ear. "God, Liv, I want to be inside you."

He took her hand and brushed it against his cock. It was like solid rock.

"Now," he murmured, his voice filled with need, as he drew her to her feet. She followed him from the pool, her insides trembling at the sight of Tempest, now sandwiched between Dom and Steele as they thrust into her, Magic stroking his cock as he watched them.

Before she could muster the courage to say anything,

Shock dragged her into the house and up the stairs. When they reached the bedroom, he closed the door, then tugged her into his arms and plundered her mouth.

But she pressed against his chest and drew back. "Shock, wait."

"What's wrong, sweetheart?" he asked, his hands around her shoulders.

"I was thinking . . . I mean . . . this would have been a good opportunity to . . ." Words failed her. What would she say? Let his friends fuck her silly?

"You wanted to stay out there and be with the other guys," he said.

She dropped her gaze, and nodded.

"Is that really what you want to do?"

She gazed up at him, biting her lip. "I thought it was something you wanted me to do."

"Don't dodge the question, Liv. Is it something *you* want to do?"

She took a deep breath. "I do. I mean, I find it a little scary, but really sexy, too. And I think it would help me."

"Help you how?" he asked, his eyes devoid of emotion.

"Shock, you've helped me so much with my sexual issues. You've been patient and tender with me. But when I go back . . . after our month is over . . . I need to be with other men."

His eyebrow arched. "Other men?"

"I mean . . . you know . . . relationships. Finding a boyfriend." She rested her hand on his arm. "I need to be comfortable having sex with someone other than you.

I think being with your friends, with you there, where I know I'll be safe . . ." She squeezed his arm. "I think it will help me."

His eyes softened. "I get it, Liv. But right this minute, I want you all to myself."

He took her hand and led her to the couch in the sitting area of the large bedroom. They sat down and he slid his arms around her and pulled her close. She leaned against him, feeling protected within his embrace.

"Liv, remember you said you wanted to do something to thank me?"

She gazed up at him in surprise. "Yes, I would." She ran her hand along his chest. "Something special."

He stared at her, his brown eyes darkening, but he hesitated.

She gazed into his somber eyes, gliding her fingertips over his muscular chest. "What is it?"

He leaned back on the couch and watched at her speculatively.

"I'm thinking of sexual role-playing."

"Of course. You know I've already agreed to do whatever you ask."

"I know, but this isn't what you'd expect."

"Whatever it is, of course I'll do it."

She wondered what it would be and how she could agree to the carte blanche she'd just given him, but this was Shock, and as much as he wanted to push her limits, he had been considerate and concerned about her feelings and fears.

"I want you to make love to me as if . . ." He hesitated.

"Yes?"

"As if you're in love with me."

Now it was her turn to hesitate. He could've asked anything of her. To be with other men, to try one of the sexual acts in the contract she'd never done . . . But this . . . she didn't understand.

"Why?"

He shrugged. "Maybe I want the 'girlfriend experience' for a change."

"Oh. Well . . . of course, if that's what you want." She leaned forward, ready to stand. "Should I go change? Pretend we were on a date?"

He took her arm and drew her close to him. "No, baby. Just right here. Show me you love me."

She drew in a deep breath, her heart beating erratically. She pushed herself onto her knees and leaned toward him, then brushed her lips on his. His breath tickled her nose as she fluttered kisses along his lips, then across his cheek, then back to his lips. She cupped his face in both her hands, loving the feel of his raspy, whisker-roughened skin against her palms and she pressed her lips to his in a light kiss. Then she deepened it.

He let her take the lead. She glided her tongue between his lips and stroked the inside of his mouth. His tongue caressed hers, then they tangled in a gentle, undulating dance. Her breath became shallow as their mouths moved on each other. She moved closer, then shifted in front of him, her knees settling on either side of his thighs as she pressed her body closer to his. His arms wound around her waist and his hands moved lightly over her back. Stroking. Her breasts crushed against his big, hard chest, her nipples swelling into tight buds.

"Oh, Shock, I want you."

"Tell me, sweetheart. Tell me how much you want me." His brown eyes bored into hers with a need she could feel in the depth of her soul.

"I want you more than life itself. You are everything to me." She kissed him again. "I love you," she breathed against his ear.

Oh, God, she'd said the words. Her heart clenched. Oh, God, she *meant* the words. She did love him. From the depths of her heart.

But she couldn't tell him that. Couldn't let him know it was true.

But this wasn't real to him. He wanted the "girlfriend experience," that was all. That gave her permission to act on her feelings without any worry that he would misinterpret and push her away. This was just playacting.

Then why did the simmering heat in his eyes seem to be filled with so much more than lust?

Clearly, wishful thinking on her part. She might not want to love him . . . but she did. And deep inside, she wanted him to love her in return.

"Show me, Liv," he murmured against her ear. "Show me how much you love me."

She nodded as she stood up and shed her pale blue, lace bra then peeled off her panties. His gaze heated her naked breasts stood in front of him, totally naked. She took his hand and drew him to his feet, then eased down his boxers. She rested her hands on his chest and let her gaze wander the length of his magnificent body with an appreciative eye. Then she led him to the bed.

She wrapped her arms around him, conscious of her hard nipples pressing against the solid heat of his body, and she kissed him. His strong arms around her, his big solid body tight against hers, made her feel feminine and soft. And the way he held her made her feel cherished.

The feeling made her want to pull away. To run and keep her heart safe.

But she needed to do this. To thank him.

And to push herself past fears she needed to set aside.

He eased onto the bed, then drew her on top of him.

She stroked his cheek, then kissed him again. She stroked his bulging bicep, admiring the Celtic star with two dragons facing each other. She kissed the inked surface, loving the feel of his rock-hard muscles beneath her lips.

She continued across the broad expanse of his chest and she found one pebble-like nipple and licked it, then took it into her mouth. She teased it with her tongue. When she suckled lightly, he groaned. She released it, gliding her thumb over it as she kissed to his other nipple, then took it in her mouth.

She could feel his erection pushing at her belly, growing larger. She glided downward, following the trail of hair down his stomach to the tip of his cock. She ran her tongue over the tip lovingly, then wrapped her hand around his hard, wide shaft.

"I love your big cock," she murmured.

She stroked his erection lovingly. "I love how it gets so long and hard because you want me."

His hand stroked over her hair. "Of course, I want you. I've wanted you since the moment I met you."

When she gazed at him, she was shaken by the depth of feeling in his eyes. If she tried, she could almost believe what she saw there was love. But she knew better than that. He wanted her, for sure. He had for a long time.

But he belonged to another woman.

That's why he'd introduced the sexual contract. So he could have her and even enjoy the "girlfriend experience," as he'd called it, without all the messy feelings to deal with. He knew what he wanted and he knew how to get it. Once they were done this month, he'd send her home, then hop on his bike and ride off into the sunset.

But, God, what she wouldn't give to have him fall in love with her.

She opened her lips and took his cockhead inside, the big, bulbous head filling her mouth. She watched his face as his eyelids closed, then opened again, revealing a deep need in his eyes.

She sucked, then glided down his enormous shaft, taking him deep into her throat. Then she glided back. Her insides heated at the thought of his big erection gliding into her. Stroking her inner passage with its solid breadth.

"Oh, God, that feels so good, Liv."

She drew back, then took him deep inside her again, to his moan of approval. After a few more times, she drew back and squeezed him in her hand as she sucked on his tip.

"Come here," he said as he took her wrists and drew her toward him.

She arched her knees over him and settled on his stomach as he drew her closer, then kissed her. His cock stirred beneath her and she raised her body. He wrapped his hand around his cock and glided it over her soaking wet slit, then pushed up slowly.

Oh, God, it was heaven feeling his cockhead stretching her as it slid inside.

Slowly, she lowered her body onto him, taking him deeper. She moaned softly as she settled on his body, his cock fully immersed in her.

He stared into her eyes, mesmerizing her.

Her whole world became the impossibly big, hard shaft inside her, and his haunting, desire-filled eyes. She lifted her body, feeling his tip dragging on the walls of her inner passage, then glided back down. Then she lifted again, lost in the depths of his eyes.

He wrapped his hands around her hips and helped guide her movements, setting the rhythm and speed.

His cock stroked her over and over in a steady, relentless rhythm. His gaze locked her into a state of intense awareness of him.

Thrilling sensations fluttered through her as he filled her again and again. Heat washed through every part of her. Her senses quivered at the exhilaration of their bodies joining with each rise and fall of her body.

"Tell me what you feel," Shock said, his gaze burning through her.

"Good." She leaned forward, her hands clutched around his shoulders. She moaned at the exquisite sensation of him filling her. "You feel so good."

"What else?"

His cock drove deep inside her.

"Ohhh . . . I . . ." She shook her head, swept up in the building pleasure.

Suddenly, he rolled them over, tucking her under his body and driving deep. "Tell me how you feel about me."

She gazed into his eyes, so filled with desire . . . and something so much deeper. "I . . ." His cock drove deep again and she moaned, then breathed the words he wanted to hear. "I love you."

He groaned and drove deep again.

Emotion and building pleasure swept through her.

"Fuck, Liv." Then he shuddered and erupted inside her.

She moaned again as bliss embraced her, shattering her control.

"Oh, God, I love you so much." She clung to him as the orgasm rocked her to her core, blasting her to pure ecstasy.

Liv's eyelids fluttered open. She was snuggled against Shock's hard chest, his big arms warm around her. Sunlight streamed in the window.

"So you love me."

She stiffened at his words, the blood draining from her face as memories of last night washed through her brain in rolling waves. Of her tangled in his arms. Of their bodies joining in sweet bliss.

Of her professing her love for him.

Oh, God, how could she have let that happen? The man was married.

But he knew she'd been playacting. He'd asked her to. He couldn't possibly believe it was real.

Except that it was. Damn it, she was totally and hopelessly in love with him.

He was a perceptive man. Maybe he'd seen the reality behind the pretense. Maybe he was worried about it. Concerned that she had fallen for him, which would make it more difficult for him to cut her loose at the end of the month.

Her heart clenched. He was a considerate man—he'd proven that in so many ways—so now he'd be worried about hurting her.

But she couldn't let him know that.

She rolled away and sat up, needing a little distance. "No, of course not."

His eyes narrowed. "What do you mean 'of course not'?"

She shrugged. "It was role-playing. You know that." She stood up and walked to the dresser, then pulled open the drawer. She grabbed a pair of panties and pulled them on.

He frowned. "It looked pretty real to me."

She slid on a bra and fastened it. "It's what you wanted, so I did my best. But don't worry"—she pulled on her T-shirt and jeans—"it was just an act."

Shock's gut clenched as he stared at her. He'd woken up in a wonderful mood, knowing the woman he loved actually loved him back. She'd said it not once, but several times last night, and that love had been crystal clear in her eyes.

Now she flatly denied it.

He stood up and pulled on some boxers and his jeans.

"So let me get this straight. You're not in love with me."

"No," she said resolutely.

He stared at her in disbelief. The word was like a stake piercing his heart, sending pain so deep into his soul he could barely breathe.

So everything they'd shared—everything he'd seen in her eyes—had all been a lie.

Anger blazed through him and his jaw clenched.

"Since we started this thing, I thought we'd grown close." His fists clenched. "I *thought* you'd started trusting me. Damn it, Liv, I have feelings for you. You must be able to fucking see that," he said through gritted teeth. "And yet you feel nothing for me."

"That's not fair," she flared back. "Especially since—"

But she broke off abruptly.

He narrowed his eyes. "Especially since what?" he demanded.

She shook her head. "It doesn't matter."

He grabbed her shoulders. "It fucking matters to me."

Her eyes widened. "Shock, please, don't make this any harder than it already is."

Fuck. He released his grip on her, then scowled. She had no idea how hard it was for him, or how much pain it caused.

Her rejection all those years ago had been torture, but this . . . now that he'd proven to her that he would always be there for her. Always protect her and her family. Yet she still didn't care for him.

"So for you this has just been about paying back the debt all along. Nothing more. This is college all over again. You don't want me now any more than you did then."

Her rejection now was a betrayal so deep, he didn't think he'd ever recover.

He turned and stormed from the room.

Liv stared at the door as it slammed behind Shock. The look of rejection in his eyes tore at her heart.

She darted across the room and pulled it open, then dashed down the stairs behind him.

She was out of breath by the time she reached the bottom, but caught up to him. No one seemed to be around.

"Shock, I'm sorry." She hurried along behind him to keep up with his long-legged stride.

He opened the French doors and continued outside onto the patio.

"I didn't mean to hurt you," she said as she followed him along the stone surface.

Suddenly, he turned toward her, his nostrils flaring, his eyes like burning embers.

"Hurt me?" The words came out stretched tight with a hard edge. He grabbed her arms and yanked her toward him. "You don't have the power to hurt me."

She felt herself dragged forward, then pulled around a corner of the house, out of view of the windows.

His eyes blazed as he glared down at her. "You're here

as my slave for one month. That's it." He pushed her hard against the wall of the house. "You signed a contract saying you'd do whatever I tell you to. If I tell you to be my fucking loving girlfriend one night, you'll do that. If I tell you to be my whore the next, then you'll do that. Right?"

His searing stare pinned her to the wall. She nodded her head, unable to utter a word.

He stepped forward, crushing his body against her, grinding his pelvis into hers. "And if I want to fuck you right here on the patio, then you'll open for me and beg for more. Right?"

She nodded.

"Answer me properly," he ground out, molten anger flaring in his eyes.

"Yes, Sir," she answered hoarsely.

He scowled, then grabbed her wrists and pushed them over her head. Pinning them with one hand, he shoved his hand under her T-shirt and squeezed her breast, then he pushed his groin forward, pressing the hard ridge of his cock against her.

The anger seething in his eyes disturbed her, but she could see past it to the hurt she'd caused him.

He released her breast and his hand slid downward, then pushed into her jeans. When he couldn't get far enough, he cursed, then unfastened the button and zipper and slid his hand under her exposed panties, curling his fingers over her mound.

Anxiety coiled through her, while at the same time his touch inflamed her. She remembered the safe word in the contract and wondered if she should use it . . . but she didn't want to.

He pushed a finger into her.

"God damn it, struggle," he grated. "I don't want some little mouse who won't stand up for herself."

She jolted her wrists against him, almost knocking him free at the suddenness of her movement, but he recovered instantly, tightening his grip. A smile curled his lips and he pushed his finger deeper into her, then ground his body against hers.

Oh, God, the feel of his finger inside her, his big, muscular body pinning her to the wall, sent her plummeting into a dark desire for more. A wanton need pulsed within her. She wanted him to take her right here.

His finger slipped from her and he pushed down one side of her jeans, then the other with his free hand, the other still holding her wrists above her head. The pants fell to her ankles.

With their gazes still locked, she felt his hand move between their bodies and heard the rustle of his jeans unfastening. Then his hard, hot cock pressed against her like a branding iron. He pushed it between her thighs, then stroked forward and back, his shaft caressing her wet folds. Her insides clenched in need.

She heard the rumbling of deep voices, then the sound of the patio doors opening. She froze. She and Shock weren't in obvious sight, but they weren't hidden either.

Through the haze of pleasure at Shock's cock stroking her intimate flesh, she could hear three male voices— Steele, Rip, and Wild Card—as they walked into the yard.

She glanced up at Shock, her eyes wide. He heard them, too, but he grabbed her right leg and lifted it, his hand under her knee, then he pressed his shaft against her opening. Then he drove inside her, impaling her against the wall.

She tried to suppress her moan at the sudden invasion, but a small sound escaped.

"What was that?" Wild Card asked from around the corner, not ten yards away.

"I didn't hear anything," Rip said.

"Like a woman . . . you know . . . moaning."

Steele chuckled. "Man, I think you've gone too long without a woman of your own. Now you're hearing things."

"True that," Wild Card responded with a laugh. "Maybe I should go in and see if Raven and Tempest are up for a threesome with me."

"Yeah?" Rip chuckled. "If they go for it, let me know. I'd love to watch."

Liv heard a splash in the pool, then another.

Shock, who had been holding her pinned to the wall, his cock buried deep inside her, began to move. As his hard flesh sent pleasure rippling through her, she glanced toward the pool. Although they were around a corner of the house from the patio, only a couple of bushes blocked them from the pool itself, and not entirely. If the men looked directly past the lush landscaping to where she and Shock were, they could catch a glimpse of them.

Shock pulled back slowly, then drove deep again, forcing another moan from her as his thick shaft stretched her passage.

•   •   •

A part of Shock wanted her to push him away. In fact, as fucking good as it felt being deep inside her, he wanted her to shove him off her and stalk away right now.

Because he knew he was being an asshole. But right now he couldn't fucking stop himself.

He nipped her earlobe and she stifled a cry, then he squeezed her nipple.

"Oh," she moaned against his ear.

Fuck, this was turning her on.

He drew back, then plunged into her again. God, she was so wet and hot. He continued to thrust, driving her body hard against the brick wall. She groaned, then nipped his ear with her teeth.

He released her wrists as he pounded into her, driving his hard shaft deep again and again. Her nails raked down his back, and her whimpers of pleasure heated his blood, driving him closer and closer to the edge. A powerful need coiled in his center, tighter and tighter. He groaned, driving harder and faster, until a blazing pleasure blasted through him, flooding his groin, then his cock erupted inside her with potent force.

As he continued to drive into her, she moaned, losing all pretense at keeping quiet, just clinging to his shoulders. He didn't even know when she'd grasped them.

Her moans of pleasure filled his ears and he kept thrusting, until they waned. He leaned against the wall, her body crushed to his, trying to catch his breath.

Finally, he drew away from her warm, soft body and strode into the house.

Fuck, he'd been mad at her, but now he was even angrier at himself. He'd fucked her without caring about her pleasure. He'd just wanted to prove to her that she was his to do whatever he wanted with. He'd wanted to convince her he didn't have feelings for her. That nothing she could do would hurt him or affect him in any way.

Now, if only that were true . . .

Liv leaned against the wall, catching her breath. She pulled on her jeans and straightened herself up, then sat on the nearby bench.

Damn it, last night he had asked her to pretend she loved him. To get the "girlfriend experience," he'd said. Just a role-playing scenario. But from his reaction this morning, she realized it had been a test of sorts. He *wanted* her to be in love with him.

But why? Damn it, the man was married!

He'd pursued her in college, but she'd turned him down. She'd done it because of what had happened to her, but he hadn't known about that. Now she'd seen just how much that rejection had affected him.

Because he was in love with her. She had seen it in his eyes.

Had he been in love with her since college?

A small hope nudged at her and she barely wanted to acknowledge it. The hope that maybe Amy had been lying to her. The photo was pretty conclusive, but maybe Shock had been married in the past, and was now divorced or widowed. She had no idea why Amy would try to convince her that he was still married, but—

"Hey, you doing okay?"

She glanced up to see Rip standing in front of her, wearing a wet bathing suit, water dripping down his legs. His muscular chest was broad and heavily inked. Every one of these men was tough-looking, incredibly sexy . . . and deeply caring.

She nodded. "I'm fine."

"You sure?"

"Yeah, thanks. Just tired."

"Why don't you come for a swim with us? That might revive you."

He held out his hand and she took it without thinking. He helped her to her feet.

"Thanks. I'm not sure about the swim."

"Come on. It's a beautiful day." His handsome face lit up with a smile. "What else are you going to do?"

That was a good question. She didn't want to go back to the bedroom. She didn't want to face Shock right now, but even if he wasn't there, she didn't want to stay holed up somewhere.

She managed a smile. "I guess."

She was a little embarrassed by the thought of facing the three men after they all must have heard her moans of pleasure, but there was nothing she could do to change that, so she'd just have to get over it. She followed him across the patio, then along a stone path to the curved pool.

Steele was sitting on the steps in the water.

"Liv's going to join us for a swim."

"Great. The water's perfect," Steele said.

She would actually love to go for a swim right now, but she didn't want to go upstairs and change because she might have to face Shock. Then she realized she didn't need to. They'd all seen her swimming in her underwear before. And these men might be big and rough-looking, but she felt safe with them. And she knew they wouldn't do anything she didn't want them to do.

She grabbed the hem of her T-shirt and pulled it over her head, tossing it onto the stone deck around the pool. Then she unzipped her jeans and pushed them to the ground, the men avidly watching her.

Liv walked to the side of the pool and dove in, then swam to the shallow end where Steele sat on the steps. Wild Card and Rip were lounging on the other side of the pool.

As soon as her feet felt the bottom, she stood up and walked toward the steps, then sat down beside Steele.

"You look like you lost your best friend," he said.

She gazed at his intense blue eyes. "I just might have."

"I saw Shock take off into the house. I take it you and he are having some problems."

She frowned and nodded.

"Don't worry. He's probably taken off on his bike to clear his head. When he gets back, I'm sure everything will be fine."

She shook her head. "I don't think so."

"I'm sure whatever problems you and Shock are having—"

"There is no Shock and me. I don't know if he told you or not, but I'm just here to repay a debt." She shrugged. "He loaned me money to help my sister, and in exchange, in addition to paying him back, I agreed to ride with him for a month. Once that month is over, I'll go home and that's that."

"Yeah, I don't believe it."

Her eyebrows lowered. "Don't believe what?"

"I'm not debating the agreement you had. I don't know anything about that. But there's no way that man is going to let you go. It's clear as day the guy's in love with you. And he has been for a very long time."

Why would Steele say those things to her if Shock was married? Because surely Steele would know . . .

Her heart fluttered. Unless Amy *had* been lying.

The woman had made Liv promise not to tell anyone she had revealed that Shock was married. She said she could lose her job if Shock found out. But this was too important. And if she was lying, Liv had to know.

She gazed intently at Steele. "Can I ask you something in confidence?"

"Shoot."

"Is Shock married?"

As soon as she saw his grim expression, her heart clenched.

"Oh. You know about that," he said.

Shock wasn't in their bedroom when she got there. She peered in the bathroom, but he wasn't there either. She sucked in a deep breath and stepped into the shower, then turned on the water. Afterward she toweled off and dressed. For the next hour she fidgeted restlessly, her thoughts a swirl of confusion.

A few hours later she heard the roar of an engine outside, coming up the long driveway to the big house.

Shock was back.

She sat on the love seat by the window, her arms wrapped tightly around her legs, rocking slightly.

She heard the front door open and close and then the rumble of male voices. Then she heard his footsteps on the stairs and a few seconds later the doorknob turned. Her gaze darted to the door as it opened.

Shock stood in the doorway, big and muscular and tough-looking in his leather jacket and worn jeans. Her heart ached at the sight of him.

His intense brown eyes met hers as he closed the door behind him.

"Liv, I want to apologize for earlier."

She nodded. "And I'm sorry, too."

He stepped farther into the room. "You have nothing to be sorry about. You only did what I asked you to do." He sighed. "But look, let's put it behind us."

He sat down in the chair across from her. "Right now, I want to do something for you."

"For me?"

He smiled, breaking the somber mood between them. "Well, I'm going to enjoy it, too." He took her hand and stroked it with his thumb. "If you agree."

"What is it?" Not that it mattered. She knew she'd do it, whatever it was.

"Well, you made a really good point earlier. That before you can really move on sexually, you should experience being with someone other than me." He grinned. "Maybe a few someones."

Her breath caught. "But I thought . . ." He'd been so adamant against it.

Excitement—and trepidation—skittered through her. But she nodded.

"Yes, Sir. Whatever you say."

Liv donned the strange outfit Shock gave her. A harness of leather straps lined with soft suede crisscrossed her torso. Straps surrounded her breasts, which were completely exposed. As she gazed at herself in the mirror, her nipples jutted forward. God, she couldn't go out in front of everyone like this. Her crotch was covered by a brief strip of soft leather, but she noticed it could be easily removed.

She sat down on the bed and grabbed one of the six-inch stiletto-heeled pumps lying in the box beside the one that had held the harness, and slipped it on her foot. It fit perfectly. Shock's personal shopper really did know his stuff. She pulled on the other shoe and stood up.

She took a few steps, ensuring she could balance on these things, then she peered in the full-length mirror again. Wow, they made her legs look long and her breasts push forward, looking fuller and sexier. She took another few steps, gaining confidence in her ability to walk in them.

Glancing at the clock, she realized it had been fifteen minutes since Shock had left the bedroom to let her prepare. He'd be back for her in five minutes. She buckled the appropriate straps around her wrists and ankles, then walked to the window and gazed outside. The sun shone brightly and the whole afternoon was ahead of them.

She heard the doorknob turn and glanced around to see the door open.

Shock's breath caught as soon as he saw her. Standing in front of the window like that, the sunlight washing over her fair skin, she looked stunning.

Her breasts, the nipples peaking forward, surrounded by the black straps, were sensational, and her perfect, curvy body fastened into the harness was a sight to behold. Her legs, already long and sexy, looked even longer and sexier in those high-heeled shoes.

He closed the door behind him and walked toward her, his cock already swelling in anticipation.

"God, you look incredibly sexy."

"I look naked," she said. Then her eyes flickered toward him and her cheeks flushed. "I'm sorry, Sir. I'm not complaining."

He chuckled. "Good. I have something else to add to your attire." He held up the collar in his hand. "Turn around and lift your hair."

She turned and grabbed her hair into a bunch, then lifted it while he wrapped the collar around her neck, then fastened it at the back. It had a series of three overlapping chains attached around the base in cascades, forming a scalloped look. A D-ring was attached to the front.

"Since you're worried about your nipples being exposed, I have something to help with that."

"You do?"

He pulled the jeweled nipple clamps from his pocket and held them up. They had black rubber on the tips for comfort, and little jewels hung from short chains on the ends. He opened one and clamped it around her erect nipple, then slid the small ring along the metal arms, tightening it.

"Oh." Her gaze darted to his.

"Does it hurt?"

"A little."

"Just a little?" He smiled. "Good."

He attached the other, tightening it to the same level of intensity. Then he grabbed the leash, which he'd hung at his belt, and attached it to the ring on her collar.

"Let's go."

Liv's nipples ached with the unfamiliar clamps pinching them. The smooth black rubber that surrounded her nipples squeezed them tightly, making them ache, but she was getting used to the sensation.

She felt a tug at her neck as Shock stepped forward. She followed him, walking carefully on the heels. When he opened the door, her stomach lurched.

Could she really do this? Walk down the stairs and onto the main floor where everyone would see her basically naked?

But the tug of the leash on her collar kept her moving forward. The heels clacked on the hardwood floor, then she was negotiating the steps in these crazy heels. Shock moved slowly, staying close in front of her, as she held on to the banister.

No one was in sight as they walked past the living room and down the hall to the kitchen. Then Shock opened the patio door and they stepped outside into the sunshine. She blinked at the change in light, then realized all five men were sitting around the teak table in the back-yard. They all glanced up as she followed Shock outside.

Oh, God, she felt so exposed.

Shock was fully dressed in jeans and a leather vest, though his tattooed chest and arms were nicely revealed. The other men wore jeans and T-shirts.

Shock leaned in close and murmured in her ear. "Raven and Tempest are willing to join us, if that would make you more comfortable."

She shook her head, knowing it would just embarrass her more for the women to see her having sex with the men.

"You sure? They can take some of the . . . uh, pres-sure."

Her gaze flickered to his. "Oh, I . . . don't know." She realized she was trembling and Shock noticed it, too.

"We'll keep that in reserve. If you decide you want them here, just let me know."

She nodded, her cheeks flaming at the knowledge that all the men were looking at her naked breasts.

"To make things easier, I'm going to take control, but if things get uncomfortable for you, remember the safe word."

He'd never reminded her of it before. In fact, he'd made it clear when they'd discussed the contract that it was up to her to remember it and use it if she needed to. He hadn't wanted to be reminded that this wasn't absolutely real.

She nodded. "I remember."

"Now, are you ready to service my friends?" he asked in a commanding tone.

Her gaze lowered to the ground. "Yes, Sir."

"Good." He tugged on the leash and led her to a rustic rectangular picnic table with attached flat benches. "Sit facing me."

She sat down, the table at her back. He leaned down and she felt his fingers at her ankle, then she heard a metallic click. She moved her ankle and a chain clinked. He attached a chain to her other ankle, too, then he tightened the chains to draw her ankles apart, opening her legs.

He reached down and tugged the strip of leather from her crotch, and she gasped, intensely aware that her intimate folds were exposed to view. The other men had followed them to the table and now stood staring at her with heat in their eyes. All of them sported growing bulges in their jeans.

"Fuck, you are one hot piece," Dom said as his gaze burrowed into her crotch.

"Dom," Shock said in an admonishing tone.

Dom lifted his gaze to her face. "Oh, sorry. You are one hot woman."

"Who wants to touch her first?" Shock asked.

Steele's eyes glinted. "I think Wild Card should have the honor. After all, he's been left in the lurch."

Liv gazed at Shock, looking for any sign of jealousy as Wild Card grinned and stepped forward.

"Yeah, my pleasure." Wild Card crouched down in front of her, a broad smile on his face, and smoothed her hair back. "*Now* we get to finish what we started."

She tried to smile, but her lips quivered. His fingers still rested on her face and he stroked her cheek with his thumb. "Don't worry. I'm sure you'll enjoy this," he murmured, low enough that the others couldn't hear. "If not, just say so."

She nodded and gave him a tremulous smile.

He stroked her neck, then his hands glided down her arms. His gaze dropped to her naked breasts, the jewels of the nipple clamps glittering in the sunshine. He flicked one of the gems, sending it swaying. Her nipple tingled.

"Very pretty." His gaze shifted back to her face. "And I don't mean the diamonds."

Wild Card cupped her breast and he lifted the weight in his hand. Then he cupped the other. His fingers were warm and gentle. He slid one hand down her side and over her thigh. When it closed in on her crotch, she held her breath. But he just traced circles with his finger on her sensitive inner thigh, about an inch from her intimate folds, sending warm sensations fluttering through her.

Then his fingers slid away and he stood up. He unzipped his jeans and his erect cock dropped forward, close to her face. It wasn't as long as Shock's, but it was impossibly wide, its tip flushed pink.

"Slave, touch him," Shock said.

"Yes, Sir."

She reached forward and wrapped her hand around his thick erection.

"Now do whatever he tells you to do."

She gazed up at Wild Card.

He grinned. "I think you know what I want."

She stroked his hard shaft, the silky skin gliding over the iron rod. His cock twitched within her grip, telling her he was enjoying this, but she knew he wanted more.

She leaned forward and pressed her mouth to his cockhead, then flicked her tongue over him, tasting the salty drop on the top.

"Oh, nice," he murmured.

She opened her lips and took his big head inside, then glided downward. She squeezed as she glided back.

"Oh, yeah."

"Hey, I'd like to get in on this action."

Dom stood beside Wild Card now, his jeans gone, his hefty cock facing her. She grasped him and stroked. He was just as thick as Wild Card, but his head was more bulbous and the area around the base was completely shaved.

"Suck me, too," Dom instructed.

She pulled free of Wild Card's cock and pressed her lips to Dom's member. His fingers coiled in her hair, and when she opened around him, he drew her close with a firm grip, feeding his cock slowly, but relentlessly into her. Just as she felt she was going to gag, he drew back, gliding out slowly.

Now Magic stood on the other side of her, his cock free and naked. She let go of Wild Card's erection and grasped Magic's. As she stroked him, Dom glided his cock in and out of her mouth. Finally, he released her and she shifted to Magic's cock. Once he was in her mouth, she moved her head back and forth on him while she stroked Wild Card and Dom with her hands.

"Hey, guys, we all want a chance." At Steele's words, all three men moved back and Steele and Rip stepped close to her.

Rip's erection was impressive. Then her gaze settled on Steele's. Oh, God, Steele had the biggest cock of them all.

She wrapped a hand around each of them and began to stroke. Her fingers couldn't even meet around Steele's giant shaft.

They were both solid as rock. She took Rip in her mouth, his cockhead big as a plum, and sucked. His groan filled her with satisfaction. Then she glided down his shaft. After a few stokes of her mouth, she slipped away, then gazed at Steele's cock, wondering how she would fit it in her mouth.

She opened—wide—and stretched her lips around his even bigger cockhead. It stretched her mouth, but she fit it inside. She began to suck him, teasing his tip with her tongue, then gliding around the ridge.

"Oh, fuck, that feels good."

She cupped his balls as she took him a little deeper, trying to get him halfway down, but failing. She glided back and sucked again.

Finally, she slipped off and returned to Rip's cock.

"Oh, yeah, honey," Rip said as he stroked her hair back.

She bobbed up and down on him for a few strokes, then pulled away to return to Steele, but before she wrapped her lips around him, Shock interrupted.

"Stop." Shock was standing beside Rip now.

Steele and Rip gave him room as he stepped in front of her and knelt down.

He stroked her face. "You're doing great, Liv." Then he leaned in and kissed her. When he released her lips, he shifted just a breath away. "Are you still okay with this?" he asked quietly.

She nuzzled his temple. "Yes, Sir," she murmured against his ear.

He eased back and smiled, then he nuzzled her neck, sending tingles through her whole body. His lips brushed lightly over her skin as he moved down her chest to her breast. He stopped and gazed at her nipple, still pinched by the clamp he'd attached earlier.

"So pretty," he said as he flicked the dangling gem. Then he tightened it.

Oh, God, it hurt . . . but felt so good at the same time. He tightened the other one and she whimpered. His gaze shifted to her face, assessing, then he smiled.

"Your nipples look so pretty pinched tight with glittering jewels hanging from them." His smile broadened. "Maybe we'll have to think about getting them pierced."

Pierced? Oh, Lord. She didn't even want to think about it. But a curious part of her wondered . . . What would it be like?

He licked the tip of one of her nipples.

Then Shock's lips were moving again. Over her stomach. She tried to move her knees together, embarrassed at the thought of him kissing her down there with the other men watching, but the chains on her ankles kept her legs spread wide.

His tongue lapped against her intimate folds in a gentle caress, dragging her entire attention to him. Then his fingers glided over her slick flesh and one slid inside her.

"Fuck, I love how wet you are."

He slid in another finger and his tongue found her clit. While the other men watched, he slid his fingers deeper into her and he teased her clit with flicking motions. Pleasure swelled within her. As he stroked her passage with his fingers, gliding deeper and faster, his tongue teasing her sensitive bud mercilessly, a haze of bliss grew around her. But, aware of the men around her, she didn't think she could let go enough to find her release.

The pleasure built within her and she leaned back against the table, arching forward, her breathing labored. Shock's hand wandered up her body, then the underside of her breast, his fingers teasing her aureole, near the tight clamp on her nipple. The barrage of pleasurable sensations was so powerful, she wanted to let herself go to the orgasm so badly . . . but she couldn't . . .

Shock's mouth left her briefly, only a breath away, and he gazed at her. "Come for me, sweetheart." Then his mouth was on her again and he suckled.

Her hold on reality slipped away and she moaned loudly as the intense sensations swept her away to a state of ecstasy.

He kept her arching and moaning for a long time, and when he finally eased up and her orgasm waned, she found herself arched backward, her head hanging over the table.

She felt fingers brushing her ankles as the chains were unfastened from her ankle straps. She sat up and gazed at

Shock's smiling face. He offered his hand and she took it, then he drew her to her feet.

"Now, slave, you will lean over the end of the table, legs wide, so we can see how wet and pretty your pussy is."

Shock guided her to the end of the table and pressed her down until she was leaning over it, resting her elbows on the rough wooden surface.

"Are you ready?" he asked.

A shiver of nervousness skittered through her, but she answered, "Yes, Sir."

She felt someone step behind her—she didn't know who—and his arm came around her waist and drew her against the hard planes of his body.

His whisker-roughened face brushed against her cheek. "It's me," Wild Card said, and she relaxed a little. Of all Shock's friends, she felt most comfortable with Wild Card.

Then his rock-hard cock brushed her slick folds and she stiffened. He glided along her slit a few times, getting her used to the feel of him, then he pressed against her opening.

"I'm going inside now." He nuzzled her ear, sending tingles down her spine. His hand cupped her breast as he eased forward slowly, his cockhead pushing inside her, hard and thick.

A little panic flickered through her as she thought about this strange man's cock pushing into her. But he wasn't a stranger. She trusted and felt safe with him.

"Are you okay?" he asked.

She drew in a couple of deep breaths as calm settled

over her again and finally she nodded. She wanted this. Wanted to feel him inside her.

She wanted to experience sex with men other than Shock. To know she wasn't afraid anymore.

"Yes." She reached her hand up and stroked his cheek. "Fuck me, Wild Card." She leaned her cheek against his. "Make me come."

He glided forward in a slow, relentless motion, filling her deeper and deeper.

She moaned at the exquisite pleasure of his shaft filling her.

He tightened his arm around her waist, his whole body pressed snug against her. "You feel so good around me."

Then his shaft filled her again. Then back. When he drove forward again, she thrust back to meet him. He picked up the pace, gliding into her again and again. She moaned as pleasure filled her. His fingers found her clit and he stroked it, sending wild pleasure careening through her.

"Oh, yes. Oh, my . . ." She choked on a moan as he drove deep and hard, then kept driving into her like a jack-hammer.

She gasped at the intensity, then quivered as an orgasm swept her away. It went on and on as Wild Card kept pounding into her, his lips nuzzling her neck. Then he jerked forward and groaned, filling her with liquid heat.

They stood there panting, him still holding her tight.

"Fuck, that was intense." Wild Card kissed her cheek and gave her one final squeeze before he stepped back.

Then Magic stepped behind her. "My turn, love." He

pressed his cock to her and pushed inside before she could react.

Since she was still in the zone, the feel of him inside her sent a haze of pleasure through her. He drew back and glided in again, then kept on in slow, steady thrusts. Within seconds she felt the familiar wave, and another orgasm washed through her. She moaned and he drove harder and faster, trying to keep up with her. Then he thrust deep and held her tight, his cock twitching inside her. Her intimate muscles tightened around him and he groaned.

Finally, he drew back, his cock falling from her. "Sweet, love. Thanks."

Then Dom stepped behind her. "It's my turn now, babe." And before she could breathe, he drove in deep. "Oh, fuck, you are so hot and tight."

Rather than shock at his sudden invasion, she felt a heady desire for more.

"Tell me you want me to fuck you," he said against her ear.

When she didn't respond right away, he tugged on the nipple clamp, sending pain jolting through her. Sweet, pleasurable pain. Then he squeezed it tighter on her nipple and she gasped.

"I asked you if you want me to fuck you?"

He kept squeezing and she groaned, then nodded. But she knew that wouldn't satisfy him, so she sucked in a breath. "Yes," she said in a hiss, wanting the pain to stop, but at the same time, to continue. "Fuck me."

He chuckled, then drew back and rammed into her again, then again. His thick cock stretched her and she cried out at the intense pleasure of him invading her over and over.

Her fingers stiffened against the wooden table, her body quivering in need. "Oh, God, yes, fuck me harder."

He drove deep, then pounded into her faster and harder.

"Say it again, baby." He grasped her throat, pulling her head back against his shoulder. "I want to hear you fucking beg."

"Please fuck me!" Her voice sounded desperate, demanding, and full of need all at the same time.

With a deep groan, he jerked forward as he released inside her.

Pleasure cascaded through her, sending her to blissful heights. She was arched back against him, taking his seed, and cried out in pleasure, while bliss swept her away to ecstasy yet again.

When Dom stepped away, Rip took his place, mounting her and then gliding inside. He rode her gently, building her pleasure until she was moaning in his arms, riding the wave to heaven.

When Steele stepped up to her, she was a bit nervous about the size of him.

Shock stepped up behind her. "Sweetheart, now it's time for something special."

"What?" she asked breathlessly. But she knew what. She was sure both men were going to take her at once.

She felt his hands glide over her ass. Then he applied something slick to her opening, sliding it around. When she felt his fingers press against her, she concentrated on relaxing. He pressed one inside her, and stroked her tight canal. After a few seconds he slipped in another finger. Then another. He was stretching her, getting her used to the invasion.

When his cockhead, also slick, bumped against her, she stiffened. He pushed forward slowly. Her opening stretched around him. A little painfully, but he was slow and steady, giving her body time to adjust. After what seemed like forever, she'd stretched wide around him and his cockhead was inside her.

He eased deeper into her and she moaned at the un-accustomed but pleasurable sensation. He kissed the back of her neck. "You feel so good around me, sweetheart."

Finally, he was all the way inside her. He held her tight against him and they stayed like that for a few moments. Then he drew her back and turned her around. He leaned against the table and Steele stepped forward.

"That's . . . pretty big," she said, eyeing Steele's enor-mous hard-on.

He chuckled. "It's okay. I'm sure you can handle it."

Then he was pushing into her vagina and she groaned at the intensity of it.

He slid in, deeper and deeper, stretching her wider than she'd ever been stretched, and filling her deeper than any cock had done before.

Then he was tight against her body, staring down at her. He smiled and kissed her lightly.

"Are you ready?"

Ready? She had a cock in her ass and another in her vagina. Sandwiched between two hot, hard, masculine bodies.

She locked onto his steel-blue gaze. "Yes, I'm ready. Fuck me."

Shock chuckled behind her and Steele pulled back. Just before he would slip free, he pushed forward again, in a long, slow stroke. Then back.

Shock grasped her hips and pressed her forward a bit, his cock sliding out a little, then he glided forward, filling her. At the same time, Steele filled her from the front.

Both men pulled back again, then drove forward together. They found a rhythm and pummeled her with pleasure. Two cocks gliding in and out. Deeper each time.

She began to moan, then the moans turned to wails. The men, relentless, kept filling her. Rock-hard shafts stretching her. Pushing her pleasure higher and higher.

It swelled through her like a tsunami and she wailed louder still as an orgasm broke through her with such intensity, she feared she would faint.

But she didn't want to miss a thing, so she held on to consciousness and rode the pleasure to the heights of forever and beyond.

The men grunted, both driving deep as hot liquid filled her and she cried out in exquisite bliss.

The three of them collapsed against the table, gasping.

"That was fucking incredible," Shock exclaimed.

She rested against him, loving the feel of the two men still inside her, their big bodies cradling her in a protective cocoon of masculine flesh.

Shock stroked her cheek. "You okay, sweetheart?"

She gazed at Steele, who was smiling down at her, and nodded in answer to Shock's question. "Oh, yeah. In fact, I was wondering when we can do it again."

Steele laughed. "Fuck, man, you definitely have a keeper here."

Liv sighed as Shock set her down on the love seat in the bedroom and pulled off her shoes. After the wild lovemaking with six men in the backyard, he had swept her into his arms and carried her here. She felt his fingers playing along her skin, unfastening the buckles holding the harness together at her back. The straps loosened and he stripped it away. Then the cuffs around her ankles and wrists, until finally all she wore was the collar.

He flicked the dangling chains holding the gems hanging from her nipples. She'd forgotten about them.

"The clamps cut off the circulation, so when they come off, the blood rushes back," he said, kneeling in front of her. "This will hurt a little, but I'm going to help. Okay?"

She nodded. He slid the little ring along the clamp to loosen it and took it off.

Pain jolted through her sensitive bud, but he quickly took her nipple in his hot, moist mouth and licked tenderly, making her forget about the pain. He suckled lightly, sending her hormones into a spin. Then he drew back.

"Better?"

She nodded, wanting his mouth on her again. "Now the other one?"

He chuckled, then gently removed that one. His mouth covered her right away, easing the pain shooting through her. She moaned softly as he licked and suckled.

Her fingers glided through his hair and she held him tight to her chest. "Thank you."

He eased back and settled on the love seat beside her, smiling warmly. "For helping with the pain?"

She laughed. "Yes. And for giving me that experience. It was incredible."

She rested her hand on his cheek and gazed into his warm brown eyes. "You know, you've already helped me in so many ways. And now I know I can be with other men, so I don't have to be afraid of getting on with my life, sexually, once this is done."

He slipped his arm around her and drew her close.

"Yeah, about that . . ." He took her hand in his, his thumb stroking her skin. "I told you I have feelings for you."

She frowned and pushed herself straighter on the leather seat. "Yes, I remember, but I don't know why you're telling me this. It doesn't change anything."

His eyebrow arched. "What do you mean it doesn't change anything?"

She drew in a deep sigh and pursed her lips. She couldn't keep this pretense going any longer. "Shock, I know you're married."

He frowned. "How do you know about that?"

Her chest constricted. Oh, God, it really was true. Although Steele had already confirmed Shock's marital status, a part of her had clung to a small hope that maybe it wasn't true.

"It doesn't matter. But I know you're married, and I know you've done these contracts with women before."

He frowned. "That's not true."

Her gaze shot to his. Had she heard him wrong the first time?

"Are you saying you're not married?" she asked.

"No. I'm saying this contract with you was special."

Her heart ached, knowing he belonged to another woman.

"Who's been telling you these things? It sure as hell wasn't one of the guys, right?"

"No, it was . . . someone else."

His eyes narrowed. "Fuck, it was Amy who told you, wasn't it?"

She looked down at her hands.

"Fuck, of course it was. Amy works at the law firm Yvette and I use. Amy is Yvette's friend. She probably found out about the contract when I had it drawn up and decided to intervene. She certainly wouldn't be happy that I'm seeing someone."

Liv was confused. "Because the two of you had an affair?"

He arched an eyebrow. "An affair? I never had an affair with her."

"But she said you had a contract with her and she started to fall for you, and she was devastated when it ended. She said she wanted to warn me that the same thing would happen to me."

His hand tightened around hers and his eyes grew intense.

"That explains why, even though I did everything I could to show you how much I care, you still thought it would end."

He squeezed her hand. "Liv, I *am* married. I'm sorry I didn't tell you that, but there was no reason to."

She drew her hand from his. "Really? I think that's a pretty important fact."

He leaned back in the love seat and sighed. "I know. I get it. Just let me explain. I met Yvette just after graduating college and we got married about a year later. Not long after that, the truth about my father and brother came out. That they were embezzling from the company. We lost all our shares in the company, and I lost all respect for them. It was tough going, both emotionally and financially, but Yvette stuck by me. She believed in me and supported me while I built a new business."

Liv's heart ached. She sounded like a wonderful, loving wife. Just what Shock deserved.

"But once I was back on top financially, I realized"—he shook his head, looking weary—"that's not where I wanted to be. I didn't want to be around all these rich people who only cared about money and power. For my own sanity, I decided to walk away from the whole thing."

"And she didn't want to?"

Shock scowled. "I can't blame her for that. I was rebellious and angry. I decided to take off on a motorcycle and live with bikers. She didn't want to don blue jeans and a leather jacket. That wasn't her style."

"Do you still love her?" Liv asked, afraid to hear the answer.

He took her hand and his intense gaze captured hers.

"No," he said simply.

Liv's heart fluttered. "Why didn't you divorce her?"

"I guess it comes down to not wanting to be a failure. My dad divorced my mother when I was very young. And even though he was very wealthy, he left her with nothing." He scowled. "My whole life I watched him go through women like tissues, and I swore to myself I wouldn't do that. That when I was in a relationship, I would make it work." He gazed at her, as if willing her to understand. "I couldn't just ditch her. So I gave her the house and a regular allowance."

"Does she think you'll go back to her someday?"

"She probably does." He shook his head. "But, believe me, that's never going to happen. Even if I stop riding and settle down one day, she's just not the right woman for me."

The way his warm brown eyes held hers made heat thrum through her.

"She's not?" Liv asked, mesmerized by the love shining in his eyes.

"No." His fingertip glided along her cheek gently, the tenderness in his eyes rocking her to the core. "You are."

At his words, joy swelled through her.

"In fact, the reality is, my feelings for her always took second place to how I felt about you." He stroked her cheek tenderly. "I never got over you."

He leaned in close. "I love you, Liv."

Then his lips swooped down on hers and he kissed her with passion. His tongue plundered her mouth and an intense yearning flared within her.

"And in case you're wondering, I've already set the divorce in motion. That's what I was doing when we went into town yesterday."

Her heart flipped as joy blossomed within her. She gazed up at him and stroked his whisker-roughened cheek.

"Oh, Shock. I love you, too."

He laughed, his face glowing. "Thank God we finally sorted that out." Then he drew her into another kiss, this one long, lingering, and oh, so sweet. When their lips parted, he stood up and walked to his jacket, which was slung over the back of the armchair near the bed. He pulled something from the pocket, then returned to her.

Then this big, tattooed, tough-looking man knelt in front of her and held up the little box in his hand. He opened it, displaying an infinity ring studded with diamonds. The sparkling gems glittered even more through the tears in her eyes.

"I'm not asking you to marry me yet. Not until the divorce is done. But this symbolizes my promise that I will." He smiled. "And I hope, when I do, you'll say yes."

She sucked in a deep breath, then let the exhilarating joy sweep through her. She flung her arms around his neck and kissed him. "Yes. Oh, my God, yes!"

Still on his knees, he pulled her from the love seat and into his arms, both of them falling onto the carpeted floor, then he rolled her onto her back and kissed her deeply. Her heart thundered in her chest, happiness pulsing through every inch of her.

He smiled. "You've already lost the ring I bought you."

She laughed and grabbed the blue velvet box, which had fallen on the carpet a foot from her head.

"Not on your life. It's right here." She handed it to him.

He opened it and found her hand, then slid the ring on her finger.

"So you agree that from now on you will love me, and *obey* me. Right?"

She grinned broadly, then grasped his raspy cheeks between her hands and kissed him again.

"Yes, Sir. Always."

Fulfill all your wildest fantasies with *Opal Carew*...

• *Twin Fantasies* • *Swing*
• *Blush* • *Six* • *Secret Ties* • *Forbidden Heat*
• *Bliss* • *Pleasure Bound* • *Total Abandon*
• *Secret Weapon* • *Insatiable* • *Illicit*
• *His to Command* • *His to Possess*
• *His to Claim* • *Riding Steele*

AVAILABLE JULY 2015 *Hard Ride*

"Beautiful erotic romance...real and powerful."

—*RT BookReviews*

St. Martin's Griffin